Finding Your Faith

Yasmin Peace Series Book 1

Finding Your Faith

Yasmin Peace Series Book 1

Stephanie Perry Moore

MOODY PUBLISHERS

CHICAGO

All Scripture quotations are taken from the King James Version.

Editor: Kathryn Hall
Interior Design: Ragont Design
Cover Design and Photography: TS Design Studio

Library of Congress Cataloging-in-Publication Data

Moore, Stephanie Perry.
    Finding your faith / Stephanie Perry Moore.
        p. cm. — (Yasmin Peace series ; bk. 1)
        Summary: Thirteen-year-old triplet Yasmin tries to find solace in prayer while helping her family recover from her older brother's suicide, as well as dealing with all of the drama of middle school and life in the projects.
    ISBN 978-0-8024-8602-8
    [1. Family problems—Fiction. 2. Interpersonal relations—Fiction. 3. Christian life—Fiction. 4. African Americans—Fiction. 5. Triplets—Fiction. 6. Brothers and sisters—Fiction. 7. Florida—Fiction.] I. Title.

PZ7.M788125Fin 2009
[Fic]—dc22

                                                              2008033130

3 5 7 9 10 8 6 4 2

Printed in the United States of America

Dedicated to
The Delta Gems & Delta Academy Girls
(programs sponsored by Delta Sigma Theta Sorority, Inc.)

Always keep the faith.
You have been equipped to succeed.
May you and every reader know that with God on your side,
you will find your way and soar!

Contents

Chapter 1

Prayer
Does Work

*G*et out! Me and my kids need some space. I'm sick of everybody trying to console us. Leave us alone." My mom was screaming at the thirty or so friends and family members that came to offer their condolences after the funeral of my oldest brother, Jeffery Jr. Everybody called him Jeff.

Everyone stopped and looked at her. However, no one moved or walked toward the door. The tension was thicker than a plump, round turkey on Thanksgiving.

"Mom, here. Have some tea," I said, trying to soothe her.

She knocked the cup from my hand sending it flying across the room. I'd never seen my mother this way.

Mom went over to the front door, opened it, and said, "Yasmin, York, Yancy, and I are going to have to find a way to deal with this. My husband is down in Orlando in jail, while we're up here in Jacksonville grieving over the loss of my oldest baby. I just don't need no busybodies coming up in here poking around. I know that most of you mean well, but right now we just need to be left alone."

Everyone quickly scurried to pick up their belongings, except my Uncle John. He was my dad's younger brother. Mom's steaming red eyes followed my uncle. He went over to my brother Yancy.

Uncle John put his hand on Yancy's shoulder and said, "Son, I need you to step up and be the man."

Yancy looked at my uncle with sad eyes and said, "Okay, Uncle John."

My mom yelled to my uncle, "If your brother had been the man, then my boys wouldn't be under so much pressure!"

"Yvette, come on now, girl. I'm just trying to do my brother's part and look out for y'all."

"John, if your brother wasn't locked up he could do his own part. Like I said, I'm tired and I just need you to leave."

"Okay, okay, Yvette," Uncle John said as he headed toward the door. "Remember, I'm only one phone call away."

As soon as Uncle John had closed the door, my brother Yancy blurted out, "I wish I could go and live with Uncle John!"

"Boy, if you don't go sit down somewhere . . ." my mother said.

My brothers went to their room while my mom went to the bedroom that she and I shared. I couldn't bear to sit inside our cramped apartment for one more second, so I went and sat on the porch.

It had been a week since my brother had taken his own life. Though things weren't perfect before Jeff's death, we had a lot of good times. We were a normal family. Now, I didn't know what we had become.

A new school year was about to begin in a couple of days and Jeff had so much going for himself. He would've started his senior year in high school—a highly recruited basketball player, one of the best in the state of Florida. All the girls liked him, but he had a strong thing going for our next-door neighbor Jada. Her brother, Myrek, was my good friend.

York, Yancy, and Yasmin. The triplets. People always asked, "What are the triplets up to? How are the triplets doing in school?" I hated being referred to as if we didn't have names and different personalities. All of us are unique, but one thing we had in common was that we all looked up to Jeff. I had no clue how we'd survive without him. I hadn't shed a tear during this whole chaotic week. My mom cried enough for all of us. York had become so angry that he was just looking for a way to relieve the craziness. Yancy was withdrawn and walked around in a daze.

Was I supposed to be the one to keep us all together? How could I? I was only a mere thirteen-year-old, headed to the eighth grade. I wasn't anywhere close to being an adult. What did I know about how to make things right? We hardly ever went to church; but my grandma, or Big Mama, as my brothers and I called her, had taught us that we should pray and have faith no matter how bad things looked.

I wanted to believe deep down in my heart that God could make this not hurt so badly. But why wasn't He making this all better? Why couldn't I wake up from this nightmare? I had no answers, just tons of questions.

I placed my severely aching head between my wobbly knees and finally released all my tears that I'd been holding back, and I prayed.

Lord, please help my family. We don't know what to do or how to keep going. I want to believe the verse that Big Mama taught me about

You, which says for me to trust in You with my whole heart and not lean to what I don't understand. But it's so hard to trust when it looks so bad, God.

Just then I heard a familiar voice. It was Myrek.

Most people call me a tomboy because I would hang out with my three brothers a lot. I usually play with the neighborhood boys too, but all summer I hadn't run with them like I used to. Actually, Myrek hadn't been playing with York and Yancy as much either. He was a great basketball player like Jeff and the two of them had been on the court most of the summer. I knew he would miss my brother as much as we would.

"Yasmin, I just came out here to sit with you."

"Thanks," I said as I wiped my face.

He continued, "I really don't know what to say. But my dad says that you don't always have to find words to say when something bad happens. Sometimes you can help people by just being with them."

"I guess that's true, Myrek, because I do feel better," I said, thinking about how I was praying when he came onto the porch.

"Cool," he said.

For the next thirty minutes we didn't say a thing. We were content just sitting in silence, occasionally looking at the sky.

I used to not care that on the first day of school I didn't have the latest clothes or sport the freshest hairdo. Going to school was all about learning, not trying to be fashionable. But as an eighth grader, somehow things had changed. Somewhere along the summer the things that once didn't matter now did.

Besides, with all that I had going on, it didn't seem right that I was focusing on material things. We didn't even have money to bury my brother. My mom had reminded Yancy, York, and me about that over and over again. Getting new school clothes was totally out of the question.

Actually, it was cool for boys to wear stuff a little roughed up, but when I looked around and saw all the girls looking fly, I hated me. My jeans that were purchased in the sixth grade and the hand-me-down tennis shoes that my brothers used to sport were a mess. Also, the braids I got before school let out last May were still in my head. I didn't look cute and I didn't feel cute; in fact, everybody that looked at me with their disapproving expressions let me know that I was not cute.

⋘⊱

"I can't believe she's coming on the first day of school looking like that," a popular girl named Perlicia said to her girlfriend Asia. "I know they live in Jefferson Projects, but even if she went to the dollar store she would look better than she does right now."

Both of them just laughed. I always found females to be so fake and phony. So hanging with my brothers and Myrek was enough for me. We always said what we felt and moved on after releasing any tension. We never held grudges and were just there for one another. Perlicia and Asia had fallen out of their friendship so many times that I didn't have enough fingers to count them.

A part of me wanted to turn around and slap them in their faces. But, what good would that do for me ending up in trouble on the first day of school? None. Both of them needed to go study somewhere. They were enrolled in remedial English.

Not that there was anything wrong with that. Myrek and York were going to be in the same class. However, why laugh at somebody when you have shortcomings too? I hated that people could be so cruel. Why did they have to add insult to injury and make me the laughingstock of our hall?

It went from one group of girls whispering about me to another one getting started. Though I never stared anyone in the face, I could feel them staring at me. Their laughter was getting on my nerves too. All of the talk just wore me down. As tough as I had always been, standing up to anyone who ever confronted me, at that moment I just couldn't take it. I dashed off to the closest girls' bathroom I could find, went into an empty stall, locked the door, and bawled.

I prayed, *I hate my life. You're supposed to be up there protecting me, making everything better. Why is it so hard? I look a mess. I feel a mess. I don't have any friends. I can't talk to my mom; she's still grieving. Can't You help me out?*

"Oh no!" I cried, realizing my monthly had just started. I could have crawled under a rock and stayed there forever. With everything going on the last couple of days I hadn't been keeping up with my cycle. Plus, this was only the fifth month. It was still new to me. Even though I had on old jeans, they were a light color. Unfortunately, as soon as I checked my pants I knew they were ruined. And the first bell had just rung. I was late for class.

Didn't You just hear me, God? I need You to help, not make it worse. What am I supposed to do now?

This must've been what Big Mama meant when she said God will direct your thoughts if you pray and ask Him. Just then, I thought about the school guidance counselor, Mrs. Newman. York and Yancy always talked about how cute she was. I remembered last year when I saw her in the hall she told me if I ever needed anything that I could come to her office. Back then I felt like I didn't have any major problems that I couldn't handle, so I never took her up on it. Now it was a different story.

After making a bootleg pad, which my mom had taught me to do in case of an emergency, I washed up and then checked the hallway. Thankfully, I was wearing one of my brother's shirts and I took it out of my pants and pulled it all the way down. I twisted my book bag toward my back so that it covered my bottom and practically sprinted to Mrs. Newman's office.

When she saw me, she quickly came from behind her desk and said, "Come in, come in. You're Yasmin Peace, right? I planned to send a note to your homeroom teacher today requesting that you stop in to see me."

I could only nod. It was hard to find words to say. On the inside and out, I was a wreck.

"Yes, and I know I'm supposed to be in class but I just need—" Then the tears started flowing.

"I know it's tough for you right now. I am so sorry about the loss of your brother Jeff. I remember him as a student here. He was a super young man."

"Well, he's gone now. He committed suicide. So what does that matter?" I muttered.

"It matters a lot," she said without hesitation. "The memories you have of him can last a lifetime. No one can take those away."

"I just don't understand why."

"Well, that's why I am here to help you. Sometimes you guys have so much on you and it feels like it's too much for you to bear."

"I mean, why would my brother do that? He knew we loved him."

"Well, Yasmin, that's a very complicated matter. I can't say for sure why your brother committed suicide. However, I can tell you that young as well as old people can feel overwhelmed—as if they have no way out of their situations. That's why it's important to talk to someone you can trust and not hold in what's going on inside."

Keeping it real, I said, "Why should I talk to you? You can't fix the problem." I was hurting, in need of healing, and didn't believe that she could fix my wounded soul.

She came over and put her hand on my shoulder and said, "Listen, I may not have the solution for you or your family, but I am here for you all to support you in whatever way I can."

"Why do you care like that?"

She gently said, "Because I'm supposed to."

I wondered what she meant by that. "Mrs. Newman, do you believe in God? I mean . . . are you a Christian?"

"Yes, Yasmin, as a matter of fact, I am. Being a Christian doesn't stop unpleasant things from happening to us or those we love, but we can become closer to God during those times. As a result, we become stronger. I can't make your pain go away, but I can walk through it with you and your family. Having faith and trusting that God will work it out can be very trying. You have made the first important step by seeking help, Yasmin. I commend you for that. You are so wise. I can tell you're more mature than most of the students in this school."

"Thank you, Mrs. Newman," I said, wiping the tears from my face and realizing that I did need her. I almost hated to ask the next question. "Just one more thing, Mrs. Newman—do you have any maxi pads?"

She went over to her drawer and said, "I sure do, Miss Yasmin." Then she handed me a decorative bag with pads and other toiletries inside. "And here are some pamphlets for you to share with your family about grief. All I have left to do is write you a pass for class, and you'll be on your way."

Having her come to my rescue was an answered prayer. Maybe God did care about little ol' me after all. I sure felt better.

Going home on the bus on the first day of school, Myrek sat beside me. I was in a daze looking out the window. Talking was the last thing I wanted to do.

"What's up, Yas?" he asked. It was obvious that he had not been able to read my body language.

I wasn't smiling. I wouldn't even look his way. I wanted to be left alone. So I didn't respond, hoping he would get that, but he didn't. He asked again after butting me in the arm.

"What's up, girl? I know you heard me." He was just like one of my brothers; I was always able to tell him everything. So it made no sense to hold stuff back and be all self-conscious about what I was feeling.

Without thinking, I just blurted out, "Boy, can't you see I don't feel like talking! I don't feel well. I'm sick of my head itching with these braids that have been in for fifty thousand years. I had an issue that made me late for my first class. Besides that, every girl in the school laughed at me today. My day was the worst first day of school ever. Any other questions?" Seems like I'd forgotten everything that Mrs. Newman had said to me earlier.

"Since when do you care about what other girls think? That's not the Yas I know."

"I don't know, Myrek, that's what's been getting me. I don't want to look so dumpy. The whole tomboy look is starting to get pretty old. In fact, if I owned some lipstick, I wouldn't mind putting it on."

"What boy you trying to look cute for?" he asked, like he cared.

I rolled my eyes at him because it wasn't really about a boy. *Where did that comment come from? Myrek is tripping,* I thought.

Defending my reasons, I uttered, "I want to be cute for *me*. I want to have style and class. Everyone thinks Mrs. Newman is beautiful and being in her presence makes me want to feel beautiful too. She's not uppity and nasty. She's fly. I don't know. Maybe I'm talking nonsense. Who wants to be cute anyway, right?"

"Oh, I think you're the cutest girl in school."

I couldn't even look at him when he said that. It felt sort of weird. Was he giving me a compliment? The guy who was always giving me such a hard time, just like my brothers, was saying nice stuff. Was he just trying to make sure that I didn't cry anymore on his watch? Like the day of the funeral when he sat out on the porch with me and talked to me like a real friend.

"It's okay, Myrek. You don't have to say nice things."

"Have I ever just said anything to you? Girls that cake all of that stuff on their faces, spray too much perfume, and wear tight clothes look stupid. I don't know; you just keep it real and I like that. You shouldn't want to change."

Finally, we were at our stop.

York said, "Y'all getting off or what? Get up."

Myrek didn't move. "You heard what I said, you shouldn't want to change. You don't understand. So I'ma help you."

"Help me? How?"

Thinking he was talking crazy for real, I pushed him out of the seat. The four of us walked from the bus stop home. Myrek didn't say another word.

An hour later, I was home alone.

Yancy went to the library. He was an honor roll student and always loved school, but now he was having a hard time with being so bright. He made straight As, but lately he was cool with getting a few Bs and lots of Cs. Most of the dudes in our neighborhood and even some at school teased him for being intelligent. He tried hard not to let folks know that it got to him.

York was hanging out in the neighborhood with his new crew that wasn't about nothing. Older boys that hung out playing loud music in their hooopties, dancing in the streets, and talking trash to everybody that walked by. York was on the verge of failing and it didn't even seem to matter to him. He barely passed to the eighth grade and his teachers said that he needed to start applying himself.

Being in the house alone was a big deal. My mom worked two jobs and came in really late. Because we shared the same bed, I didn't get much space on my side. Just to lie in the bed alone was so relaxing. I saw a couple of dresses hanging on her side of the closet and wondered how they'd look on me. I hopped up, put them against me, and looked in the mirror. I longed for a new look. I wanted to look at myself and like what I saw. A knock at the door disturbed my fantasy moment.

It was Myrek. *What did he want?*

"Hey, hey. Open up," Myrek said. "My sister wants to talk to you."

Jada used to be over here constantly with Jeff. Somewhere along the summer, they fell out with each other. Jeff seemed sad after that. *Why did she want to see me though?*

"What . . . what's going on?" I said as I opened the door.

"Okay, I'ma leave the two of you alone. I told you that I was going to help you, Yasmin," Myrek said before dashing away.

"What is he talking about, Jada?"

She came into the house with two big suitcases. "I'm gonna give you a makeover. I owe that much to Jeffery to do that for you. Myrek was telling me that you want to be gorgeous. You don't want to look like a tomboy. 'Bout time, girl!"

"Jada, I'm not sure if I want a makeover. I mean, I don't want to look phony."

"Whatever. Let's get these braids out of your hair, slap a perm in it, and hook you up. I have tons of clothes that are going to fit you. Ooh! You are going to be so cute."

"I don't have any money to pay you for anything."

"Girl, you don't need to pay me. I like doin' this kind of stuff. Plus, when people see how different you look, they'll ask who did your hair and stuff. It'll be good advertisement for me. I could make money on the side doin' this! You're Jeff's sister and we're like family. I need to do this. I loved him, you know."

As she jerked my head to the left and to the right taking out my braids, I endured the pain with anticipation. I didn't know how the makeover was going to turn out, but I was overjoyed about the possibility of a change. If God sent her, if this was His way of helping me, I was grateful. I certainly had put in enough requests, asking Him daily to make my life easier. I guess I had the answer to my question: Prayer does work!

Chapter 2

Expresser
of Emotion

*M*y new look was bangin'. Jada layered my hair with a few brown highlights to make my new do pop. All of her hand-me-downs looked good on me. She had a lot of stuff that even looked brand-new. People were definitely going to be paying attention to Yasmin Peace! It felt real good to be confident.

My mom was gone before we left for school, so she didn't even get to see the new me. My brothers—well, let's just say I was the last person York and Yancy were paying attention to. Quite the contrary. As soon as I dashed onto the bus after almost missing it, Myrek slid over, showing all his pearly whites.

He said, "WOW! Jada told me I was going to be surprised, but you look . . . Man, girl, I didn't know you was gon' look like that."

I had never had a boy look at me in any other way than someone to toss the ball to. For Myrek to be able to smile and not take his eyes off of me—just felt different.

When we pulled up to the school, he asked me, "Whose class do you have first? I'll walk you there."

"You don't have to."

"I want to."

Getting off the bus, I said, "Look, I owe you a real BIG THANK YOU! I was really down about my appearance. You stepped in, in a big way, but I'm still the same old Yasmin. We're still boys."

"Looking at you, how could I ever think of you as my buddy again? I mean, you've got curves and stuff."

"I also have a big brother that'll beat you—"

What was I thinking? I didn't have Jeff anymore. I was so caught up in having a new outfit, hairdo, and totally new appearance. Jeff was gone; when was I going to get that through my big skull? I felt guilty for enjoying my makeover.

I held my hand out and made a stop motion to Myrek; at the same time I started to run as far away from him as I could. I knew he would say that it was okay and that I still needed time to get over it. I also knew he'd try to make me feel better, but my brother was gone. Nothing could make me feel better, not a new hairdo or clothes. On top of that, I wasn't used to wearing heels. When I ran down the hall, I stepped the wrong way and the left heel came off my shoe. I was so frustrated that I sat down on the floor next to my locker.

Why did Jeff have to leave? Why did this have to happen to my family? Why couldn't God help him through his depression? Why did my father have to be in jail? I had so many questions going through my mind. Then the two mean girls, Asia and Perlicia, interrupted my thoughts.

Asia said, "Mmm . . . hmm. She got her hair done, but it'll be a hot mess soon."

"I wonder where she got that cute outfit from. Did you see her yesterday?" Perlicia remarked. "You wear your best stuff on the first day. Everybody knows that. Why does she look like a beauty queen today?"

Asia said, "Maybe she's been dipping in that money everybody has been giving her family since her brother died, or maybe there was some kind of insurance on him. That's why my grandma said she wasn't going to take none out on herself because if we got the money we would just throw it away. Can you believe her brother committed suicide in the first place, how stupid!"

Okay, enough of the pity party, I thought. No way could I continue feeling sorry for myself. Yeah, it was one thing for them to talk about me. I could handle that. However, for them to say something about my brother, calling his act stupid . . . what gave them the right?

"Okay, you two are talking a little too much stuff right now. Yesterday I let you guys talk about me as if I wasn't nearby. But I heard you. I have a lot on me right now. I am not the one to mess with! So what if I want to put on a dress, fix my hair, and look cute. It's my business how I look when I come to school. Why do you have to be all in my business trying to figure out where the money is coming from? You ain't give it to me. Or, do I need to help you stay in your place?" I let the tomboy in me come out, putting my fists in front of both of their faces.

Myrek came in between us and said, "Hey, there you are."

Both of them got all giddy and silly. All of a sudden, they went from dissin' me to throwing themselves at Myrek.

"Myrek, hey. It's me, Asia. Don't you remember me?"

The other crazy girl competed with her so-called friend. "No, he remembers me, Perlicia. We were in a couple of classes together last year. I'm a cheerleader this year. I'll be yelling the loudest when you score your three-pointers. Shoot! Shoot!"

He gave them a half wave and then turned back toward me. "I was worried about you. You just ran off."

"I've gotta go to class. Myrek, I can handle me. Why don't you just stay here and talk to your groupies. I'm out."

I changed my shoes and put on the gym shoes that I had in my locker and then went to class. I was stressed. I was mad. Even in my most pitiful moment, I had to get backup. Figure out a way to maintain pride. This thing I was feeling was between me and God. Only He could help me through it. Forget everybody else.

Two weeks passed and I was beginning to hate school. Not for any reason in particular. Well, I guess there was a reason and it wasn't academics. Though I didn't consider myself an Einstein, the work that I'd done so far was a piece of cake. My teachers were cool. I wasn't sure if everyone knew what had recently happened in my family and had begun taking pity on me, but they all seemed overly nice.

It wasn't that I was tired in the mornings. I didn't even have to get up extra early. This year, school started thirty minutes later than it usually did.

It was probably because I was a loner for most of the day. As tough as I tried to be, who wouldn't want a friend? But a girlfriend? I wouldn't know where to start. But somehow I didn't feel comfortable hanging with the boys anymore.

When I got to my homeroom, Miss Bennett, who happens to

be my Algebra and homeroom teacher, said, "Yasmin, you're just the person I've been looking for, come here."

"Me? . . . why?"

"Yasmin, this is our new student, Veida Hatchett. I'd like for you to let her shadow you since you young ladies have most of the same classes."

The next thing I knew, I saw this girl with light skin like mine, with pretty hair and hazel eyes. She was all smiles.

"Hi, Yasmin. Thanks for letting me hang with you. Again, I'm Veida," she said as she extended her hand.

She had a French manicure and her teeth were perfectly straight. I wish I had the money for braces, though my doctor said I didn't need to have them straightened for one crooked tooth. She even had on some sweet-smelling perfume. Veida was very well put together. I wanted to compliment her, but I didn't know how.

So I was taken aback when she complimented me out of the blue. "You look like a model. I wish I had your height. I'd really be a model then." She didn't care how it sounded. She had no problem saying something nice to me. It was so cool.

I was sort of tall; well, not sort of—really tall. I looked down at most girls and intimidated most boys because I could look at the majority of them eye to eye.

"Thanks!" I was really humbled over her thinking that I had it going on.

"Wow, why are you looking at me like that?" she asked, not keeping any of her thoughts inside.

I liked this girl. She shot straight at it. She wanted to know something, so she asked me. No phoniness. No foolishness. Veida just kept it real.

"I hadn't figured out a way to tell you that you were cool and cute and all that stuff. But I don't know . . . me and conversations, it's hard."

She said, "Well, I know what you mean. It's hard to say to another girl that you think she looks cute or that you like what she's wearing. But my mom says that girls need to support each other more. And since it's my first day, I don't know anybody at this school—and that's really hard. So I'm going to need you to introduce me to all of your friends."

This Veida girl was going on and on, but I liked it. She was real about what she was feeling.

"Uhh . . . If you want someone to introduce you to people, you've got the wrong person. I don't have any friends here. Particularly, no friends of the female persuasion."

"I should have known!"

I couldn't believe she said that. Did it look like nobody liked me? Did it look like I couldn't hold down a friend? I just gave her a puzzled look.

"Oh, no! I mean, I should have known because you're cool. You've got it going on. I had friends at my old school but they fell off one by one because girls are so jealous. Girls can be so mean and tear each other down. So it doesn't surprise me that girls hate on you."

"To be quite honest, this girly stuff is new for me. I'm a tomboy. My mom works all of the time and I hang with my brothers."

"You've got brothers? I wish I had a brother. I have an older sister who gets on my *last* nerve! How many brothers do you have?"

She kept going on and on so much about her sister that I think she forgot that I hadn't responded.

"Wait, Yasmin, weren't you telling me about your family?"

Well, Lord, I thought. *You know I was thinking about having a true girlfriend. Do I stay closed up? Do I scare her off and let her know that I'm grieving and make her feel obligated to be my friend. Yet, if I keep it to myself and not say anything, what kind of relationship are we truly able to start? Either she likes me for who I truly am or she doesn't.*

"Veida, I had three brothers."

"Okay, you said *had.* What do you mean? Are they like step-brothers and stuff where they lived with you and now they live with your dad or something? 'Cause I forgot to mention that I have a stepsister too, but that's a whole 'nother story."

"No, no. I'm a triplet. It's me and two boys."

"Aww, that's so cool!"

"But, I had an older brother too, and he died a couple of weeks ago."

"Oh . . . um . . . what happened to him?"

"I really don't want to talk about it—not right now . . . not here."

"Oh, I understand. I know it must be really hard for you. I am *so* sorry. I've never had anyone close to me die."

She didn't even know me and yet she was feeling my pain. Wow! Was I dreaming?

Before I knew it, the tears started, releasing what I tried to hide. I wanted Jeff back, but I also wanted a good friend. I knew the jury was still out on whether Veida and I could be tight buddies. Still, I silently thanked God because maybe He was giving me a true friend—not to replace my brother—but because He knew I needed one.

◦✦◦

I didn't really know how to be a strong Christian, but Big Mama always said that if I prayed with a sincere heart, the Lord would hear me. Over the last ten days, He'd done just that. Veida and I were really becoming tight. It didn't matter to me that I didn't have a bunch of girlfriends. I had opened up to Veida so much: before school, during school, after school, during change of classes, and at lunch. I told her stuff I thought I'd never share with anyone.

"I hate Algebra," she said after Miss Bennett handed back our first major test. "I don't even know why I'm taking it now. I wanted to wait until the ninth grade, but NO! My mom wanted me to take it this year and you see this big 41 percent. What can I do with that, Yasmin?"

I was feeling good when I saw my 98 percent, but I didn't want to show it to her and make her feel worse.

Veida shook her head assuming mine was bad as well. "Is your score this low? This stuff was hard, huh?"

"I don't want to show it to you."

She snatched it from my hand. "An A, ugh. I'm such a dummy!" Tears welled up in her eyes.

I wouldn't say she was overdramatic, but it didn't take much for her to cry. I felt bad that she had flunked the test.

"I'll help you." I told her. "Ask Miss Bennett if you can take it again. It's the weekend. If you study, you can get this."

"How can we study together if we live in two different parts of town?" Veida asked.

"If she'll let you retake the test we'll figure something out."

That's all I had to say. Veida hopped out of her seat and headed over to Miss Bennett's desk to plead her case, like a debate team member. Then she came skipping back over to her seat with a huge grin.

"She said all I need to do is study and she'll let me retake it on Monday. Yas, how'd you know?"

"I figured since you're new most teachers would try to work with you."

At lunchtime Veida whipped out her phone and started dialing. When I tried to ask her something she put up an index finger and shushed me. What was she doing? I guess she either didn't know or care that her cell phone could be confiscated for being used in school.

"Hey, Daddy. Can I go over to my friend Yasmin's house so she can help me study for a big exam I have on Monday? I'm gonna ride the school bus with her. I'll text you the address later. Thanks, Daddy. Love you. Smooches."

"Wait, wait, wait," I said with attitude as she ended the call. "I haven't asked my mom and plus you don't have a note. You can't just get on the bus with me. I don't know what it was like at the school you transferred from, but if they catch you using your phone here, they'll take it and give you a detention!"

"Yasmin, please. I don't get caught. Anyway, I have a good reason, right? I have to let my parents know and how else can I do it if I don't call ahead of time?"

I guess she was right about asking her parents ahead of time. But the part about not getting caught, Big Mama always said that you might not get caught doing something every time, but that eventually your sin would find you out.

"My dad can handle the bus thing. If it makes you feel any better, I'll text him right now and tell him to call the school ASAP

. . . There, it's done. If it's such a big deal, why don't you call your mom and ask her?"

I didn't know how to tell Veida that I didn't have a cell phone. The more I thought about it, she was an upscale, rich girl. I was poor and from the projects. I wasn't sad about it, but I wasn't trying to parade her in my home. Though we had talked about a lot, I hadn't let her in on the fact that me and my mom shared a bedroom.

In a state of panic, I said, "No, you can't come to my house."

Thankfully, the bell rang and I got my stuff and went out to the hallway. We usually walked together, but I didn't need to be around Veida right now. Unfortunately, she caught up to me.

"Look, Veida," I said, not beating around the bush, "I live in the projects. I don't know if that's a problem for you, but it is what it is."

"Girl, please, my cousins live in the projects. That's not a big deal. I'm not trippin' on that. I don't want to be your friend because of where you live, and I hope you know that I would never judge you. If we're really cool, it shouldn't matter where we live."

Then she pouted her lips out and gave me a pitiful puppy-dog glare. "Okay?"

Reluctantly giving in, I said, "Okay."

The school day flew by. I was sort of nervous bringing her home without permission. But my mom would be at work and it was for a good reason. After all, I had to help Veida with her math grade.

"Who is this fine hottie on the bus?" York yelled, unable to take his bulging eyes off my friend.

"There is nobody different on this bus," Yancy said, hitting him in his arm until he looked up and saw Veida sitting beside me.

Yancy stared like he knew her. She batted her light hazel eyes back at him. What had I missed?

It never occurred to me that both of them would lose their minds when they laid eyes on her. I guess we never ran into each other because York was in remedial classes and Yancy had honors classes. The two of them were so silly, trying to beat the other down the narrow bus aisle to get to where we were sitting.

"Yancy, move, boy!" York said, elbowing him back. "Sis, introduce me; who is this?"

York picked up Veida's hand and tried to kiss it. Before he could, she yanked her hand back. Then Yancy shoved him into the back of the bus.

"Y'all need to sit down back there!" The bus driver wasn't playing.

"Those must be your twin brothers."

We're triplets! I thought, but I just nodded my head at that point. I didn't even want to claim the two of them acting like idiots. Then I saw Myrek step onto the bus. I just waited for him to come over and drool too, but he didn't. He smiled when he spoke to me, politely smiled at Veida, and then sat down.

"Who is that guy checking you out?" Veida said to me.

"It's just my next-door neighbor."

"Oh, that's the guy you've been telling me about. Hmm . . . I won't say nothing."

"There's nothing to say," I replied as we both laughed.

When we got off the bus, I was stunned to see my mom's car. She was at home. I hoped she hadn't gotten fired because it made no sense for her to be home in the middle of the day.

Running into the house, I saw her on the couch and said, "Mom, what's wrong?"

"I'm tired, girl! That's what's wrong!" She saw Veida behind me. "I know you ain't got no company. This house ain't cleaned up. I just want to rest."

"Hi, Ms. Peace, I'm so sorry to just show up here. It's my fault. I'm not doing good in Algebra and I asked Yasmin to tutor me. My dad is going to come and pick me up as soon as we finish. I promise I won't get in the way. I could help her clean up, if that's okay?"

"Clean up? Well, come on, girl. You talkin' my language. See, Yasmin, that's how you need to be. Where are your brothers? Tell them to get in this house now. Come on here, girl, and tell me about yourself. Come to think of it, I've never met a girlfriend of Yasmin's."

When I stepped outside, I couldn't believe my brothers were fighting. York was on top of Yancy. Yancy had his hands around York's neck.

"Y'all step back," Myrek said, trying unsuccessfully to push them apart. "Over a girl, this is stupid."

"Nah, I saw her first and then he gon' try and rap to her. She ain't trying to be with no nerd," York said.

"At least I've got something going on. And who said you saw her first? She's here so Yasmin can tutor her. She ain't interested in sixth-grade classes, dummy," Yancy said, pushing him back.

"Why does everything have to be so messed up? I hate it here," I yelled.

Lately, I had been real sad a lot and kept everything to myself. But I was no longer going to hold stuff in, letting them think that their actions didn't affect me. Their little fight wasn't just about Veida. They were hurting inside because of Jeff's suicide and my dad being in jail too. They needed to own up to what was going on with them, reach deep inside like I did, and be an expresser of emotion.

Chapter 3

Matter
of Fact

"*B*oys, what is all this noise?" Mom came out on the porch and the door slammed behind her. Seeing her sons fighting, she said, "What the—"

"Ma!" I screamed cutting her off before she could embarrass me in front of my new friend.

"Look, Yasmin Peace, I'm grown. I can say whatever I wanna say, how I wanna say it, and when I want to say it. Now what's goin' on out here?"

My brothers got up and dusted themselves off. They weren't saying anything.

"York, Yancy, y'all better start talking! And, Myrek, you looking just as silly as they are. What's going on? Like I don't have enough to deal with right now. I came home because I had a headache and wasn't feeling good. I'm not gon' be bothered with this mess."

"It was just a misunderstandin', Ma," York huffed and finally said.

"Boy, if it was just a misunderstandin'—" She couldn't even finish her thought. Mom just fueled up and grabbed York by his collar, "Then you wouldn't be out here fighting like some thug. I know it was you who started it."

"You always take his side, Ma. Just because I don't bring As in the house, you think I'm some no-good hood rat. You already lost one son. What, you want me to run away too, huh?"

She just looked at him and rolled her eyes. Their exchange was more intense than the one my brothers were having.

"Cool, you ain't gotta worry about me coming back," York said as he blew past our angry mother, dashed in the house, and started grabbing some stuff.

Yancy went over to Veida who was looking shocked. I didn't even realize she was standing in the doorway. I wished my brothers had kept it down so my mom wouldn't have heard them.

Mom said, "So that's what all of this is about? I'm standing here fussing with your brother because I think he's giving you drama and this is all over some girl? Yasmin, you should have known. You need to check with me when you want to have company. Oh, and don't you start with no tears. You know what I'm talking about. These little fast middle-school girls." She uttered that last part under her breath, as if Veida was the cause of the boys losing their minds.

Actually, my mom might not have finished high school, but she was street-smart. Veida *was* the cause of the tension between my brothers. But on the other hand, it wasn't like she was flirting with them or playing them both—the way that I see some girls do to boys to make them jealous.

York was huffing and puffing when he came back outside.

Myrek tried to talk to him, but he stepped off the porch. I knew York was deeply hurt.

My mom went over to him and said, "I'm sorry, York. I don't need no attitude from you. I misjudged the situation. I know it was both of y'all. You know I love you, boy."

"Whatever, Ma, you always take his side. I just need to jet for a bit. Come on, Myrek," York said as he headed next door.

"I'm sorry, Miss Peace. You want me to tell York to come back?" Myrek asked my mom to let her know that he wasn't supporting York's behavior.

"Gon' boy, he can cool off with you. Just as long as I don't have to worry about him messing with this gang that's hanging around here vandalizing everybody's property. I'm cooking; once he starts smelling my greens he'll be home," Mom said.

"Ms. Peace I am so sorry too," Veida chimed in. "I don't know what happened. I was just with Yasmin. Like I said earlier, I'm just here to get tutoring for Algebra."

My mom looked her up and down, smacked her lips, and said, "All right, I'm going to give you the benefit of the doubt. I'm so used to these little girls around here playing one guy over the other. My sons just don't need no tension over no girl. You supposed to be studying with Yasmin, gon' and study."

"I can help her, Mom! I did my homework in class," Yancy stepped up and said.

"Yasmin can help her own friend. If it's somethin' she don't understand, then Yasmin can come and get you."

"Yasmin, do you have some homework of your own to do?" I nodded in response to Mom's question.

"Then, do that first and then you can help Veida. Gon' in there, sit at the table, and study. And oh, push my greens to the side. I'll put them in the pot in a second. Let me go check the mail."

"Ma, can I talk to you?" I said, following her with my hand on my hip.

I hated to admit it, but York had a point. Mom thought whatever Yancy did was the best. She loved athletics and she loved academics. But now since Jeff was gone, I guess she was just going to hop in line with whatever Yancy said and make it happen.

Mom frowned as she looked at the bunch of bills she was holding. "Yes, Yasmin. What's going on, girl?"

"I don't know, Ma, it's like we never talk anymore. You say you've got a headache. And I understand you're drained because of Jeff and everything, but we haven't even talked about it. It's like you're taking out all of your frustrations on me and York."

"Yancy gets his grades. He stays out of my way. He even cleaned up the room so I wouldn't have to go in there and get down on my knees to clean up my own son's blood. And what do you and York do? You keep our room messy. York runs the streets. I don't talk to you anymore? Yasmin, when I do talk to you, you half do what I say."

"Ma, but I've been trying to put stuff up."

"Quit whining, Yasmin. You should have checked with me before bringing company over. You're not gonna try and twist stuff around like I'm the one with the problem."

"Ma, it's not like I have a cell phone to call you. I didn't even know you were home. And we never talked about company."

"Oh! So you're trying to just sneak around and do what you want to do, twisting what you know I'd want. You know bringing a girl over here when I'm not home is the wrong idea. You are thirteen years old, with thirteen-year-old brothers. Friends of yours are not allowed to come and go as they please, particularly when I'm not here. Anything can happen with you teenagers and your ragin' hormones.

"The only one who has ever had that privilege to be here when I'm not here is Myrek and that's because I've known his little self since he was in diapers. Now that I see how he's looking at you with this new hairdo of yours, his visits might have to be cut out.

"Y'all kids think I'm crazy. That's just a part of it. I didn't poke my nose into Jeff's business more and he just—Ughhh! I can't even talk to you right now."

"Mom, do you even love me?" I said to her as she walked to the front door.

"Yasmin, this is the wrong time to try and play on my emotions," she said as she turned around and looked at me.

Life in the Peace household was anything but peaceful.

Thirty minutes later, Veida packed up her stuff. She was so busy getting her book bag together that she didn't even see that I was extremely sad. Yancy kept coming in the kitchen to watch us study and Veida obviously enjoyed the attention, constantly giggling and making eyes at him.

"My dad just called. He's almost here."

I couldn't even look at her. I thought we had a good friendship. But she had paid more attention to Yancy than to what I had been saying.

"So, you're mad at me?" Veida finally realized.

"Duh! It was like you were trying to start a conflict in my family."

"No, I just figured that I would go with the flow. I actually think Yancy is really cool, though. Please don't be mad at me."

Her dad pulled up in the shiniest, black Mercedes Benz I had ever seen. I didn't have anything to say to her. I just waved.

Then the dark-tinted window rolled down and her father said, "You must be Yasmin?"

"Yes, sir," I responded halfheartedly, really not wanting to carry on a big conversation.

"Well, thank you for helping Veida out. She was very apprehensive about her new school at first. Lately, all she's been talking about is her new girlfriend. Yasmin, you're welcome over anytime. Okay, hon?"

"Yes, sir," I uttered, again half-interested.

"Thanks, Yas," Veida said before letting her window up.

I couldn't even be fake anymore. I was so happy when they drove off. I felt like York because I wanted to get away too. I had three dollars in my pocket and the corner store was down the street. I figured I'd just go walking. It wouldn't be like my mom would worry or care. Maybe a cold Mountain Dew would get me over my woes.

Fall was in full effect. The breeze that hit my face was refreshing and I was enjoying it. But then I ran into Tyrone, or "Bone," as he liked to be called, and two of his thug friends. Instantly, I felt knots in my stomach. I wanted to turn around and walk the other way, but I had to pass by where they were standing.

"Oh, look who we have here," Bone said as he licked his lips. "My girl, Jada, said you was cute. How did you know that I was about to come visit you, girl?"

He was all up in my face. When I tried to walk to the left he blocked me. I tried to walk to the right. He was there too.

"Can I just get by?" I said, knowing that now I could no longer ignore him and simply pass.

Like a slick snake, he eased his yucky cologne-smelling self over to me.

"You can get by after we have our little chat."

"A chat?" I said, "I have to get to the store."

One of his sidekicks said, "Man, leave her alone."

"Naw, Jeff owed me and this little . . . she gon' pay up," Bone said, squinting his eyes at me.

I had no idea what he was talking about. How did my brother owe him anything? I wanted to go off on him and give him a piece of my mind. However, I knew I had to chill. Bone and his boys carried weapons. It was three of them and one of me. He was messing up the neighborhood by bullying people, breaking into folks' houses, and doing a bunch of other stuff that wasn't right.

Some people said that he was the reason that Jeff and Jada had broken up. I didn't really know and couldn't understand why Jada would be interested in him. I'd never seen her with Bone but the rumor was that they were kickin' it now.

Almost whispering, I said, "Bone, I am going to say it again. Please get out of my way."

"She said *please*," one of the dudes said, mocking me.

"Slim, shut up." Bone threw the gum from his mouth to Slim.

Slim and Bone. Ugh. Just being around them irritated me. I wanted my mom bad. I guess this is what I got for just running off.

Standing up for myself, I said, "I don't owe you nothin', okay?"

"Yeah, you do. Your brother owed me. I lost big when they won that championship game."

"That was dumb. Jeff was great. Who told you to bet against him anyway?" I said and immediately wished I could take back my smart tone.

Bone looked at his boys. "Aww, she's a big girl with a big mouth! But since you think you're all *CSI*, your brother and I had an agreement. He was supposed to lose the game. I lost money because he didn't."

I looked at him like he'd lost the little sense he had. "Well, he's dead—"

"Yeah, but you can work for me and earn it."

"Work for you? . . . I don't think so!"

"Your brother was weak. Jada left him for a real man."

I didn't know who I'd tell or what I'd do next, but I wasn't going to do anything for Bone. Once dismissed from his presence, I ran home.

≪◈≫

It was the last weekend in September. I couldn't believe the week had flown by so quickly.

I had actually gone back to being a loner and I liked it. Veida tried to talk to me, but I wasn't crazy. I saw her meeting with Yancy every now and then even though York had never mentioned it anymore. They had a rule in the house—no girl was going to divide them. Yet the two of them couldn't even have harmony anymore after what happened over Veida.

I held her responsible. If Veida couldn't sense on her own that she needed to stay away from Yancy, then why would I want to maintain a friendship with someone so selfish?

Asia and Perlicia had been leaving me alone too. I could only focus on my work and pray that Bone's threat was just talk. I couldn't talk to my mom about it; either she'd freak out and try to take matters into her own hands, or she would go to the police. For a while there were even rumors that Bone had some dirty cops on his side. Even though it seemed like trouble followed him, it was more like Bone and his crew had been watching too much TV.

As I thought more about my conversation with Bone, he was just gonna have to get in line and take a number because he wasn't the only problem in my life.

Yeah, I was so glad it was Friday. With the weekend upon me, I could just relax and chill, which was something I was looking forward to. I had checked out a big juicy novel from the library and couldn't wait to get into it. As soon as I got out of my sixth-period class though, Myrek stepped up to me.

"Hey, you headed to the bus?" he asked.

I couldn't believe he had managed to get a little smile out of me. Frankly, all the crazy talk about him liking me was creepin' me out. The whole week I'd purposely been distancing myself from him. However, even as I pushed him away he was still nice to me. After a long week of not really talking to anybody, I really appreciated that.

I decided to ask him about something that was bugging me. "Myrek, is Bone Jada's boyfriend?"

"Yas, she says that they're just friends, but I don't know. I told her he ain't nothin' but trouble. But you know how some girls can be. They don't like nice guys, just ones that they think are hard."

Speaking of how "some girls" can be, before I could respond, Perlicia and Asia stepped in between us. One of them put her arm through Myrek's left arm and the other cuddled on his right side.

They just ignored me as if I wasn't standing there at all.

"Myrek, are you going to the football game tonight?" Asia asked, puckering her lips like she wanted to blow a kiss.

Perlicia didn't even let him answer; instead she used her finger to turn his cheek toward her. "Or maybe you're going to the movies?"

They were so stupid. They made it so obvious how desperate they were. My eyes rolled so hard.

"Hey, y'all," he said to them as he stepped back, "I was walking with Yasmin."

While he was apologizing, I tuned out the rest because I was becoming more and more upset. I mean, he was a true gentleman and a real cool dude. He didn't need to be nice to them rude chicks.

So I said, "You see he's trying to get away, why y'all still standing around him?"

"We can do what we wanna do," Asia said.

"Myrek isn't interested in a tomboy anyway," Perlicia added.

"I don't think he's interested in airheads either," I said to the both of them.

Myrek chuckled.

Perlicia added, "All you want to do is be his friend. He doesn't need some little project girl."

Myrek got serious. "Wait, hold up. That's where I live too. If y'all got issues with that, then y'all really have issues with me!"

"No, no, no. We're just saying you need to be around girls who are polished," Perlicia pathetically tried to take her extra-wide foot out of her mouth.

"If you are so 'polished' your nails would be done," I said to her as she quickly covered up her nails with their blue chipped polish.

"If you had any class about you, you wouldn't be begging a guy to hang out with you," she jabbed back as if we were in a word match.

"Begging? Ain't nobody desperate but you and Asia. Myrek has been my friend since forever and I don't have to chase after him. That's beneath me!"

"Yeah, whatever," Asia said.

With confidence, I said, "He'd be hanging out with me before he'd hang out with you guys any day. Come on, Myrek." I grabbed his hand and we left both of them standing there.

"See, I told you she likes him," I heard Perlicia say as they walked behind us.

"But he doesn't like her," Asia said.

Myrek stopped and turned around and said, "I do like Yasmin Peace, as a matter of fact."

Chapter 4

Whatever I Got

We were standing in the hallway after Myrek had just announced that he liked me. I wasn't one to be speechless, but at that moment, someone could have picked my chin up from the floor. That's how much my mouth was open. I couldn't believe he liked me . . . where was this coming from? We'd been friends forever.

"I think you like me too," Myrek said boldly.

I swallowed hard. Now I had to respond. So I gave him a weird look like *why in the world do you think that?*

He said, "'Cause you didn't want me talking to either one of those girls."

"Oh, please. I just did what I had to. It seemed like you didn't want to hurt their feelings, so I stepped up and took care of it. Plus, they're no good for you. Airheads and high-maintenance girls are not for you. You need someone to talk to—not phony girls but real friends—"

"Like YOU!" he cut in and said.

"What are the two of you looking so weird for?" Yancy said, stepping between us. "Yas, have you seen Veida?"

Finally melting from my awkward moment with Myrek, I said, "Why would I be looking for her?"

"Oh, you mad because Veida and I are hanging out?"

"No," I said, slightly irritated.

Myrek and Yancy looked at each other and nodded. Like they knew what I was feeling. I could have socked them both.

"You need to get some business of your own," Yancy said to me, jarring Myrek in his side. "Can you help me out with that, Myrek?"

It was like Yancy knew something. I wondered if Myrek had told my brother about his so-called feelings for me. If so, Yancy seemed cool with it.

Then we heard York yell, "You better get out my face, man!"

His voice was coming from around the corner so we couldn't see what was going on. However, we definitely knew it wasn't good. I was so sick of drama.

"That's York!" Myrek said as he and Yancy took off.

Yancy and Myrek were the laid-back ones. It was York and I that always found ourselves in trouble. If someone came to York or me with a bunch of junk, we weren't going to take it. We were hot-heads and even though I didn't know what was going on, I knew York was probably just protecting himself.

"What? What you got to say now?" York said as he got up in some seventh grader's face. Myrek and Yancy pulled him away just in time. "Let me go, let me go! I'm tired of him always talking 'bout my clothes. So what 'cause I ain't got no name-brand stuff on. He ain't talking now that I shut him up."

"What are you thinking?" Yancy said as he popped my brother on top of the head.

"Yeah, you better be glad no teacher or anybody came through here and heard you goin' off. You'd be in detention, or worse, suspended," Myrek added.

The little seventh grader ran away fast from the whole situation. York wanted to go after him, but Yancy and Myrek contained him. It was hard for me to see myself calmed down after someone riled me all up, but looking at York's veins popping out of his neck showed me that his anger had gotten the best of him. So whatever I needed to do to get him to chill needed to happen quickly—before he got himself into some trouble that he wouldn't be able to get out of.

I mean, our dad was already in jail. Although I remember talking with York and Yancy about us never doing anything to get ourselves locked up, that conversation took place in the fifth grade. Now that we were older York hadn't figured out a way to control himself.

"Y'all just don't understand; get your hands off of me, Yancy! Myrek, get back," York said intensely, pacing back and forth.

"Look, we've got to make it to the bus," I said to the three of them. "Come on, York. You can't fight everybody who says something about you that you don't like. That boy is a seventh grader and you're an eighth grader who wants to graduate. You don't need to get suspended over something stupid."

"Yeah, he made some little comment to one of his friends. I'm just tired of it. I know I been wearing these jeans over and over again, but this is all I got. He better just stay out of my business. So what if we don't have it goin' on with money. He's lucky y'all came."

"No," Yancy said, "you'd better be glad we came too. Ma keeps telling you about your hot head. And you got more pairs of regular jeans. You just like to wear the ones with stripes down the side. You could have gotten three pair for that one."

"So what if I want to wear the ones that I look good in?" York defended.

"Yeah, but you know people were going to have something to say about you wearing the same stuff over again," Myrek said timidly, trying not to rile York up even more.

"Whatever, man. So I'm gonna do what I gotta do so I can buy myself what I want. I'm tired of comments and I'm tired of washing my clothes every night. I've got to get the money from somewhere."

York walked out of the building and headed to the bus. His last statement really got to me.

Just what is he really willing to do? He wasn't old enough to get a job. I was worried.

"Boy, come here, Yancy!" Mom screamed as her irate voice filled the apartment.

York and I looked at each other wondering what he could have done to make our mom so upset. It was so out of character for her to be yelling at Yancy that York and I had to be nosey and find out what was up. So we dashed toward the bedroom and peeked into the doorway, trying not to get caught.

"Yancy, explain this grade to me. I could have gotten a 20 percent and I didn't even graduate high school. This is ridiculous, Son. York makes better grades than this. You're an honor student."

"Ma, I need to get into some lower classes. I told you I didn't want to sign up for those honors classes anyway," Yancy said. "Every time I turn around it's heavy homework in Literature."

"Well, I don't see how you got an F. Did you study? Did you know what Shakespeare was talking about? Answer me! I know you did."

"I don't know," Yancy answered.

"He wanted to flunk," York leaned over and whispered to me.

Though I knew it too, I didn't want that to be the case. He was the smartest thing in the house.

"Well, that little allowance you get?" Mom cut in and said. "I don't know about that . . . on second thought, you're not getting it next month."

Yancy put his head on her shoulder. "Ma, come on now. You don't understand what kind of pressure I have on me."

"Pressure?" she said, jerking her shoulder to remove him. "You don't know nothin' 'bout pressure. I work two jobs just to make ends meet for this household. Feeding y'all and putting clothes on y'all's backs. And you know how York is; he can't wear just anything."

"You got that right," York said a little too loudly.

"And, you two," Mom said after turning toward the door, "need to go somewhere else. I'm talking to Yancy. The house might not be that big, but we got more than one room. Get out of that doorway!"

We pulled back in a hurry. But even though we knew what our mom meant about eavesdropping, we were being hardheaded and couldn't resist. So we stood quietly in the hallway and continued listening.

"Ma, I just want to get out of honors classes altogether."

"Now, boy, you gon' give me a reason. Is the work too hard? Or are you just not applying yourself? Because if you can't handle the work, then you need to turn off that video game, leave that music alone, quit thinking about them knuckleheaded girls, and pick up the book."

"So, just because I can do it means I have to?" Yancy spoke with passion.

"Of course!" she responded just as passionately.

"You don't understand, Ma." He stormed out of the room.

"Boy, I ain't finished talking to you!" Mom yelled back.

Yancy blew past us. Before we could get up and out of her way, we were caught.

"Didn't I tell you two to go somewhere? That's half y'all's problem. Always minding someone else's business and can't mind your own. Turn that TV off and do some homework, 'cause if he making twenties, I hate to see what y'all would bring home."

"Ma, you ain't even listening to the boy," York said after Yancy slammed the front door to go outside. "He can do it. He just don't want to. I don't see why you're making him take honors classes anyway."

"Same reason I am making you take the remedial classes even though they were going to pass you on. Some folks need extra help. That's you. Some folks can't go on to the next thing if they ain't mastered what they had last quarter. Some people who already have that will become bored without a challenge.

"That boy has got a chance to be a doctor if he wants. But he has to stay on track. And stay on track with those who are on track to be doctors. If I let him get off course now because the work is too hard or because he didn't want to today . . . I've got to stay on him," she said as she eyed both York and me.

I understood at that moment where she was coming from. Though she had a lot going on, she still wanted to keep pushing. The smirk on York's face told me he was jealous of Mom's concern for Yancy.

She touched York's face. "I've got to push all of y'all so you can have better options than I had. So if I have to be a nag, if I have to put my foot on your necks, if I've got to take away everything up in here that y'all like other than schoolwork, then I'll do it. The Peace kids are gonna make it."

My mom shed a few tears; then York hugged her. My heart felt good for the first time in a long time.

I slipped outside to find Yancy. I walked to the front and didn't see him. Hoping he wasn't far, I looked in the back and saw him.

"Come on, Yas, I'm tired," Yancy uttered when he saw me coming toward him.

"I just want to know what's going on. None of this makes sense to me. You can do the work but you don't want to. I would kill to take honors classes."

"No need for me to talk to you. You're not going to understand."

"What?" I asked.

He said, "Girls don't like the smart guys or the nice guys."

Wanting to whack him, I said, "This is about girls?"

"Yeah. I'm not a punk. Just because I get good grades they all look at me like I'm some nerd or something. I want to be down and cool like Myrek and York. But because I don't split verbs, walk cool, and take remedial classes, I don't get respect from the crowd. I don't know; the best thing I've got going for me in the threat department is that I live in the projects. Some people won't mess with me because they think I'm tough just because of my address. I need more respect than that."

"Aww, Yancy," I said to my brother as I tapped him on the chest. "I look up to you. You help a lot of people. You even helped Veida with her Algebra."

"But I want to take classes with her. She's in the classes with all of those other guys. They get to spend more time with her than me. So maybe if I'm not in honors classes she and I can really kick it, you know?"

"So, you're trying to get kicked out? Yancy, you're not stupid but that idea sure is."

"I told you, you wouldn't understand. This is how I feel. I don't want to be on that fast track anymore with just the nerdy kids. They've been my friends for years and that's cool and all, but I'm into something different now. We're separating. It's places where they want to go and hang out but my folks aren't there. You know what I'm saying?"

"I know what you're saying, but still . . ."

"I ain't trying to hear it, Yas. My mind is made up. You just do you and I'm going to do me."

"You're missing a lot of them shots," I said to Myrek. As I passed the neighborhood playground, I noticed he had missed several baskets in a row.

It was the first time I had really opened my mouth and talked to him in weeks. I was a little embarrassed to know that he liked me. I knew I had feelings inside of me for him as well, but I didn't know what to do with all of that. So I stayed away. I sat in the front of the bus when I saw him in the back with my brothers. In the hallways when I saw him coming in my direction, I turned around or headed toward the restroom.

I said, "Hey, what's going on with you? You missed some shots. You can do that blindfolded."

Dropping his head, he said, "I don't think I have it anymore."

"What do you mean, you don't think you have it anymore?" I said, not buying his excuse at all. "I know you, Myrek; the only person that could beat you was Jeff."

"Well, maybe that's it. Now that he's gone maybe I don't want to play."

"No, what's really going on?"

"I just don't want to play it anymore, okay?" he said, getting testy with me and walking away.

"Wait, Myrek, don't walk away. Why are you acting all strange?"

"Playing is a lot of pressure. I don't know if Jeff ever talked to you about all his basketball woes."

"Sometimes he said it was hard and I know he worked with a tutor to bring his grades up. He just went out there and did his thing. He had scholarship offers after winning the state title."

"Yeah, but he gave up, Yasmin, and I know he was strong. Thinking about it messes me all up."

I didn't want my friend to feel like he couldn't make it or didn't have what it takes just because of what happened to Jeff. I couldn't do anything about Jeff being gone, but I could do something about Myrek feeling like he had to carry it all. He was just in the eighth grade.

"You've got time before you hit high school."

"Well, to go pro is one of my goals, but it's not realistic. Do you know that only one out of one million boys gets to play in the NBA?"

"Wow! I didn't know that."

"So basically my chances are slim to none! And if I can't shoot for the things that I really want then I might as well give up now. I need to figure out something else to make my father proud. All he cares about now is me getting out on that court and dribbling. He didn't make it and now I have to. He thinks I'm our ticket out of here. And I'm not smart like Yancy. I have to find a way to enjoy school more or I'm not going to have anything going for myself."

"But you have basketball. You're great at it. If you don't go to the NBA you always have college. You will make yourself into something."

"It's just a lot of pressure, you don't understand. I just don't want to play anymore right now. Everybody is looking at me like I'm supposed to be the one to bring them out of their gloom by winning a game or scoring a three-point shot. It's just more than I want to handle. And the girl that I'm interested in isn't impressed with my skills anyway."

"Well, if I didn't care about you, then I wouldn't be here talking to you. Unless you were talking about Asia and Perlicia."

"No, not them girls. They would be the first ones to not be in my corner after a loss."

"Exactly. We're true friends. I'm not going to be there because of how you play. I'm going to push you if you don't do your best, but you wouldn't expect less from me would you?"

"No."

"I meant what I said earlier. You're good and you could be good at anything. That includes school stuff. I'm not the brightest, but I do good. It's because when I don't understand it, I go to the teacher just like you go to the coach for help. You can go to your teacher if you need help on something. Try to be the teacher's pet," I said jokingly.

Myrek smirked. "I'm not kissing up to anybody."

"You can call it whatever you want. It works. You have to let the teacher know that you're trying. You may not be the smartest or the best but you have to keep trying. We have a great counselor at school, Mrs. Newman, that you can talk to. She's helping me right now. Myrek, you have the skills. Just go for it."

"I hear you, Yasmin. I want to be better at school and basketball. So I've got to use whatever I got."

Chapter 5

Stranger Things Happened

My mom was at her second job. I was writing in my journal before drifting off to sleep. Surprisingly, Yancy came in and sat on the bed. I didn't know if it was because we were triplets or just because I had been living with York and Yancy for so long that I knew when they were being mischievous.

So I stopped writing and said, "All right, what do you need?"

"See, why I always need something?" Yancy said, delaying his point.

"Can't you see I'm having some 'me' time?"

"Well, that's your problem. You're stuck with just yourself. If you had a girlfriend to share it all with you wouldn't have to write it all down."

"Yancy, don't try and act all tough. You have a journal somewhere."

He snarled, "I wrote in it when I was eight, but I don't write in one anymore."

"What do you want?" I asked, making it clear that he was aggravating me at that point.

"My girl, Veida."

"What about her?" I said, giving him the ugliest look ever.

"She misses you. She wants to be friends. She wants to talk to you. And umm . . . for me, can't you call her up and talk to her?"

Question after question rolled from my tongue: "Are you kidding? You must be joking. Have you lost your mind? There is no way that I am calling her. She chose the Peace family member she wanted to be connected with. I have nothing to say to her."

He kept pleading his case. Frustrated, I got out of the bed and slammed the door to the connecting bathroom.

"Call her," I said out loud to myself, as I looked into the mirror.

No way, I thought. Even though I did miss the girl, without her I had less stress. It was hard for me to believe we hadn't talked in a month. Although we had classes together, we sat on opposite ends. I made sure we had our seats changed right away after we had our verbal altercation. She could do whatever she wanted. She could be with whomever she wanted. Call her; that was a joke.

Then the phone rang and Yancy knocked on the door. He said, "Here, it's for you."

"Yancy, I'm busy."

"Here. Take the phone. Talk."

I knew it was Veida. Since I didn't want to call her, he had her call me. I took a deep breath, opened the door, and grabbed the phone from him.

"Hello," I said, sounding irritated and hoping that she would get the point that I didn't want to talk to her.

"Hey," she said timidly.

"Yeah," I said to her in a way like "get to the point." I mean, I didn't have time to hold her hand. She chose her course so she had to live with the consequences. We had suffered severe drama in our family because York and Yancy both liked her. And seeing all of that, she was still in touch with one of them. She threw our friendship completely out the window.

"What do you have to say to me, Veida?" I uttered, being really agitated after replaying it all again in my mind.

"I'm sorry. I'm really, really sorry," she said to me. "I didn't want to like your brother and in the process I've lost a great girlfriend. I just want my friend back."

I had never heard someone apologize to me so sincerely.

I prayed before I even answered Veida. *Lord, please help me with this. You know I miss her. Obviously she knows how bad she hurt me. Am I supposed to accept and believe in her apology and try this friendship again, or was it all a mistake? Lord, she did me wrong once. If I let her back into my world and she lets me down again, it will be shame on me. She chose Yancy over me. I don't want to compete with my brother for my best friend's attention. But Yancy's right; I'm writing way too much in my journal. Obviously, I needed to talk to You.*

"Hello, are you there—Yasmin?"

Knowing that God gives grace and that I mess up sometimes, I said, "We're cool. Let's just talk tomorrow at school."

"Cool. You just don't understand, Yasmin. I miss you and I can't wait to talk to you at school. I've got so much to tell you."

"Okay." I had to admit, it did feel good letting that anger go.

When I got to school the next day, I walked past Mrs. Newman's office and she asked me to come in for a minute. We hadn't had a heart-to-heart talk since she helped me out on the first day of school. I gladly went to sit in her office.

"I just wanted to see how you are doing. You were on my heart and I wanted to make sure you are okay," she said.

"Actually, I'm okay. Just wondering why God makes some people struggle."

"Sweetheart, everyone struggles. Some just struggle harder than others."

"So why would a loving God have His people struggle so much? Why is life so hard?"

"If everything was perfect, why would we need Him? He loves us and He knows what's best for us, Yasmin. However, we've got to know and believe in faith that He is working everything else out for the good, even when we lose a loved one."

"Is He punishing us when we lose someone we love?"

"No, He gives everyone a free will. What we do with our lives is our choice. I know it's hard for you to understand. But we are to love Him more than anything and any person. Even though things happen that may be out of our control and we don't understand why, we've got to trust Him."

I heard what she was saying and somehow through her words, I felt that God had a plan for my family. I only wished that Jeff could've felt like there was hope for him no matter what he faced. My brothers, my mom, and I just had to keep holding on, knowing that the Lord would definitely work things out.

That afternoon when I met up with Veida, I was overwhelmed when she placed her arms around me at lunchtime. I thought she was exaggerating or something about missing me so much.

"I missed you, Yasmin." Then she hugged me a second time.

"Okay, okay. I got it," I said, feeling a little uncomfortable; I mean, I was not used to the closeness. I didn't want to push her away but I didn't want to be smothered either. Sensing that I was a little distant, Veida questioned me.

"I see it's going to take a lot for you to forgive me, huh?"

I just looked up at the ceiling, and then I played with my spaghetti. She stared me down, waiting on a response.

"Come on, Yasmin, talk to me. Or do I need to keep talking to you and giving you more information so that you'll understand?"

Frustrated, I uttered, "What can you possibly do to help me understand why you ditched me for my brother? You didn't even know him."

"Actually, I did know Yancy from gym class. When I dropped some stuff from my bag, everyone else walked by like they didn't see it. He was the only one kind enough to pick it up. Then that day I saw him getting on the bus, I got goose bumps."

"You mean, you liked my brother before you even knew he was my brother?"

"Yes, I guess that's what I'm trying to say. When he fought with your other brother I felt horrible. I didn't want to pick him over you, but you gave me no choice. It was like if I didn't stop talking to him you would stop talking to me. I was torn because this was the first time I ever felt like I really liked a guy. I don't know, I guess I got too excited."

I put my fork down and turned toward her to give her my full and complete attention.

"I like hanging out with Yancy. He's one of the first boys that I have ever been cool with, but he is not you. The deep talks that you and I had don't even compare to what happens when I talk to him. You were the one person I could come to and be me. I was no one's daughter or sister, I was just Veida. I miss our girl talks. You're the best thing about this move, and I'll do whatever I can to make this right. I even told Yancy that."

"So wait, wait. So now, if I tell you not to talk to Yancy anymore, you'll change your mind?"

"I don't want to. But it's not like your brother's my boyfriend or anything. He's just a good friend. I've been a little down. He's cool with us being that close, he says he'll wait until you're ready."

"Well, I can't do that. If Yancy's happy with you as his friend, I don't want to stop that."

"Well, will you be my friend again? Does it have to be either or?"

I reached out and hugged her. That was so far beyond me, but it actually felt good. So I said, "Honestly, I miss you too."

We started back right where we had left off a month ago. We were walking to class daily. We were talking about everything. We wanted to hang out. She had even gotten her mom to call my mom to ask if I could go to the mall with them the next Saturday. Veida wanted to be a model and the mall was having open auditions for a department store's upcoming fashion show.

When we got to the mall, Veida said, "I am so nervous. Having you here with me will help a lot."

"I'm here to support you, girl. You'll be *America's Next Top Model*," I said, giggling.

She was the cutest little thing to be so short. I towered over her. She wanted to model despite her size and I told her that just like they have plus-sized models, they should have cool, short ones too. It isn't about how tall you are; it's about how you work the runway.

Nervously, she said, "Well, show me that move, I don't know what to do."

"All you've got to do is put your hands on your hips," I said in the dressing room area as I started strutting. "Prance and bring your hands up high, keep your head up high, and work it, girl."

I didn't even realize people were watching me. When I stopped walking, I got a lot of applause.

"Okay, Yasmin, my mom is calling me over to that information table where the other models are gathering. Watch me walk over there. Then give me a thumbs-up if I did it right."

"All right."

Veida did a good job and I put both thumbs up. She and the other models were getting information from another lady who was helping with the audition.

Just then, this cute, professional-looking, young blonde lady came up to me.

"Hi, I'm Theresa Hall, the owner of Young Models Inc. Are you going to try out for the fashion show today?"

Bashfully, I said, "Oh, no. I'm here with my friend Veida. The pretty girl right over there. She is fabulous and wants to be a model. I hope you pick her for the fashion show."

"Well, she is adorable," Miss Hall said as she looked across the room at Veida. "But I am very interested in your unique look. I'd love to see you in the show. Seriously."

"No, no. I can't do that. I'm with her," I said, trying to get the attention off of me.

She came closer and said, "Listen, sweetie, some people just have what it takes to be a model. I very rarely see it and I see you have what it takes. The gig is going to pay. Take my card. You don't have to audition today. You're in the show. Just give me a call. What's your name?"

"I'm Yasmin Peace."

"Aww, how pretty. Yasmin Peace, please give me a call."

Veida came back to where I was. She didn't know what was up. She looked at me as if to say "thank you so much for helping me get an edge." I felt bad. I tried pushing *her*, but the lady wanted me. It was so weird; it was too much. Did I want to be a model, and if I did, how would Veida take it? I thought, *Oh, this is crazy!*

"My mom is never going to agree for me to spend the night," I said to Veida as her mom called my mother after our mall outing.

"Leave it to me; my mom is so good with this kind of stuff. She always gets my sister's friends to spend the night. I never have anyone over, so it's my turn."

When Mrs. Hatchett hung up the phone, she said, "Your mom said it's okay. I'm going to swing you over there for your stuff."

"I told you!" Veida screamed. "We have all night and you have to tell me everything that lady said about me today at the mall. I can't believe I have to wait on them to call the people who made the show."

I would have loved to see what Veida's house looked like. From how she described it, I could imagine how beautiful it was. However, she was putting pressure on me about something I knew I couldn't come through with. So I quickly started thinking that I'd better not go at all.

"I don't want you guys to go out of your way to drop me back off tomorrow. That's . . . that's okay, we can do it another time."

"No, sweetie, your mom said it's okay. We'll wait while you go and get your things."

I tarried as I got out of the car. When we got to the porch, Yancy was at the door. I knew he wasn't trying to greet me; after all, I'm just his sister.

"You can't go and speak to her," I said to him. "She's waiting with her mom in the car."

"Man, Yasmin! Just tell her that I said hey."

I gave him a crazy look. I wasn't his messenger. I walked around him to get my stuff.

He followed me and said, "So, you're spending the night over there. Wow! You know, she lives in a mansion."

"Yancy, please."

"Tell me if she talks about me tonight."

"She talks about you all the time, you know that," I said to him as I shoved him out of the way.

Before my mom came out to meet Mrs. Hatchett, she said to me, "Now, girl, you know that I don't like it when you have parents asking me if you can spend the night somewhere. We don't spend the night nowhere. Shoot, I wanted to tell the lady no and she just wouldn't let me. Every excuse I gave she came up with something else. These people live in a good neighborhood?"

"Ma, they live in Westbury."

"Oh, my goodness. Well, you know how to behave yourself, Yasmin."

"Yes, ma'am."

"I'll be at work tomorrow when they bring you home, but your brothers will be here. Don't try to call me and ask if you can stay longer. Have her bring you home, you hear?"

"Yes, ma'am," I said, detesting that I had to hear what I already knew.

"Excuse me?" she asked when she saw that I had an attitude.

"Sorry, Ma."

"Don't act crazy," she said, lightly swatting me on the bottom. "She said that I didn't have to give you no money, so I guess you'll be all right. And you didn't invite yourself to stay over there, did you?"

I didn't huff, but I wanted to. "No, Ma."

"All right, I don't want you getting over there and wishing we had this and that. 'Cause if it's going to be about all of that, then you just need to stay here."

"No, I would never do that, Ma."

Walking to the car with me, Mom said, "All right, well . . . have fun."

Mrs. Hatchett rolled down the window and talked with my mom for a minute and then we took off.

I guess Yancy and Veida were trying to be sensitive to me because Veida didn't ask to come with me to get my stuff. Yancy didn't force the issue either.

Her mom took us to a fancy restaurant for dinner. Her father and older sister joined us. Watching the four of them was really interesting. They didn't carry on a conversation. Everybody just ate and it was sort of dull. They just didn't seem close like my family. I wasn't judging them; I just found it to be odd because at my family's table we couldn't get enough words in. Particularly when Jeff had been there, all of us were cramming to say something.

Veida had everything: money, a mom, and a dad. Why did they look so unhappy? Did they know how blessed they were? I couldn't tell it if they did.

I was so happy when we got to her house. It looked like something straight off of a TV show. It was gorgeous. We had to go through a gate to get in and the house had a circular driveway with a four-car garage. I couldn't even imagine what the inside looked like.

But what I did imagine only paled in comparison to the real thing.

"I'll take you to my room first and then we can pop some popcorn. I'm so glad you're here," Veida said.

I couldn't believe she had her own suite. Not only did she not have to share her bathroom with her sister, but she had her own bonus room too. It was like a whole side of the house was hers. It was awesome.

When she took me around the whole house, I was so amazed. The countertops in their kitchen sparkled; she told me they were granite. The wooden floor was so beautiful that it made me not even want to step on it. She said the shine was permanent. They even had a pool in the backyard. I couldn't wait until summer. I wouldn't have to go to the YMCA; I could just come over to her house and take a dip.

"Keyshia is on the other side of the house. Ughh, she makes me sick. I don't even want to take you over to her side."

"Why do you detest your sister so much?"

"Because she's spoiled and she always gets what she wants. Most times she has my parents arguing over her and I just . . . I don't like how she treats me; she's mean."

"Yeah, well, me and my brothers have it out a lot too," I said.

Veida said, "Yeah, but at least you guys care about each other. Keyshia is too selfish to care about anyone but herself."

I pray that changes, I thought.

After the tour was over, she said, "So, that's the house, but now we have to talk about what the lady said."

My stomach dropped. I wished she'd forgotten. I started gritting my teeth.

"What, why don't you want to tell me? I've been asking you all night, Yasmin."

"But, we haven't been alone. We've only been at dinner or in the car—"

"Okay, well now we're alone," she cut me off and said, "tell me."

I took a deep breath. I didn't want to break her heart. A good friend just couldn't do that.

"What, what's wrong? What did she say? I saw you pointing at me."

Since Veida and I had just gotten things back together, I knew things were still too vulnerable between us. But we had to be honest with each other. So I didn't know how to break the news, and I didn't want to lose what we were building.

"Why won't you tell me, Yasmin; I didn't make it?"

"No, no. I don't know all of that."

"Well, what did she tell you about me?"

"See that's the thing; she didn't want to talk about you." I went over and sat on her bed; she followed and sat beside me.

"You can tell me anything. If she said I was horrible or too short to be in her show, just tell me. I can handle it. I'll just work harder for the next one."

I finally blurted it out, "No, it wasn't anything like that. She said that she wanted me in the show."

"You?"

"Yeah, she watched me work the pretend runway and she said that she liked my style. I'm sorry." I looked away.

"Are you kidding? This is great. You should be a model. You're beautiful and if you get in, then you can help me even more."

I guess she really was a cool friend. I was all stressed over thinking she was going to be mad. Yet our chat wasn't like that at all.

"You know, you've really got it made, Veida," I said to her as I looked around at her gorgeous place. "We live in a rat hole compared to this place."

"Whatever. You've got it made too."

"What do you mean?" I asked.

"Your family is so close. You guys talk to each other. And Yancy can't stop talking about you and York. We don't have that closeness. Maybe if we lived close together instead of all over this big house, we'd have what you guys do."

I couldn't believe that as much as I admired her, she admired me back. Little Veida had such a powerful heart. It seemed strange that she wasn't upset with me about the modeling opportunity. Strange too, that I didn't let my stubbornness get the best of me by not giving Veida another chance. I guess it was good that stranger things happened.

Chapter 6

Worrier by Default

*I*t was now the middle of October. It was Thursday and Veida had been absent for the past three days. The first day I didn't think anything about it. The second day I was concerned. Then I called her several times but got no answer. I was over the top with worry when Yancy told me he couldn't get her either. It wasn't like I had a car to drive over and find out if she was okay. So when the fourth day came, all I could do was pray.

I prayed, *Lord, Veida is in Your hands. It's not like her to not reach out to me. I haven't seen her in days. I hope everything is all right. Please take care of her, in Jesus' name. Amen.*

"Can we sit down here with you?" I heard a familiar voice ask, just before I bit into my cheeseburger.

I was really confused when I looked up and saw Asia and Perlicia with their trays, wanting to join me at lunchtime. I gave them one of the craziest looks I could even make. Why would they think I would eat lunch with them? We never got along. We never talked to each other. Why would they even want to eat lunch with me? They never had anything nice to say about me. So when I tried to ignore them, they shocked me even more by sitting down.

Asia said, "You look really cute today. You have on a sweater that I saw in the mall last week. I like it a lot."

Veida's mom had bought it for me when we went to the mall. I was digging my outfit too, but I didn't want to acknowledge that to Asia. Actually, I appreciated her compliment.

Before I could figure out why she was being so nice, Perlicia started with more nice words. "And your hair is so cute."

"You know," Asia said, "we have been so wrong by pushing your buttons and being mean to you. We're all eighth graders headed to high school next year and we should get along."

Did they think I was crazy? Get along for what? For them to make a fool of me?

"Y'all, I was just trying to eat my lunch here," I said, feeling real uncomfortable with sitting between the two of them.

They wouldn't stop talking. One said something nice, and then the other would say something. It was like they were playing "being nice Ping-Pong." I was not going to be the ball any longer. So I decided to cut to the chase and lay all the cards on the table.

So I asked, "What's up, ladies? This isn't who you are. I hear apologies, but I don't think they're sincere."

"Wait, wait . . . don't be offended; we are sincere," Asia said.

"Yeah," Perlicia added.

"Wait a minute." I quickly got up from my seat. "We've never been nice to each other, and we don't need to be girlfriends. I actually like it the other way, okay?"

I tried to pick up my tray to leave the table, but Asia grabbed my wrist. "Please, can you sit down? Give us a chance?"

I hated that I couldn't take them at face value. I just didn't believe they were on the up and up. I knew that the world would be a better place if more folks just got along, but some things are just apples and onions. They may be round, but they don't taste the same.

I took Asia's hand off my wrist gently, and said, "It was good talkin' to y'all, but I'm out."

Because it was seventy degrees in Florida, we could also eat outside on the blacktop. As soon as I found a good spot on a picnic table, I sat down. Unfortunately, those two were right behind me.

"Did y'all not get what I said?"

"Maybe you didn't understand us," Perlicia insisted, not waiting for an invitation.

"Why do y'all want to be my friends now?"

"We just told you—we think you're cool. We're all too big for that petty stuff," Asia said.

"Well, we don't have to argue. We don't have to be cool either. I could say hey from a distance. I'm not getting up and moving anymore, but I do want some time by myself. Can you guys just leave?"

My mom taught me that you can't trust people when they change so abruptly because that usually means they have ulterior motives. Saying one thing, but not saying what's really going on. Those two weren't slick. They couldn't con me. But they were not giving up. They were trying to prove they cared. *Why is it so important to them?* I wondered. I refused to move and they wouldn't leave either, so the three of us ate together—for the first time ever.

That wasn't even the end of it. Later that evening when I was at home doing homework, the phone rang. I was so excited because I figured it was Veida. However, I was quite disappointed to hear Asia's voice saying hello instead.

"Hey," I answered in a not-too-thrilled tone.

"It's not just me. Perlicia is here too. We're calling three-way."

"Yep, Perlicia here. Hey, girl."

"I'm doing homework. I didn't even know y'all had my number."

"We've always had your number. We would call and hang up sometimes," Perlicia said.

"Shhhh!" Asia said to her. "What do we have to do to let you know we are serious about the three of us hanging out?"

"It doesn't matter what you guys do," I said without thinking. "I don't want to hang out with you."

"Is that really nice? Is that really the Christian attitude to have?" Asia asked. That stopped me right in my tracks. Why would she say that to me? I never knew her to act Christian-like. After all, they had been so mean. Was I supposed to forgive? Faith was about trusting the things you can't see, believing in things you don't have evidence for. I wasn't always nice to them either.

"All right, yeah, y'all . . . let's try the friendship thing. I'll see y'all at school tomorrow. I gotta get back to my homework now."

"Great!" Asia said. "We'll see you right in front of the office at 8:15 sharp.

"Bye, diva," Asia said to me.

"Yeah. Bye, diva," Perlicia chimed in.

I hung up the phone only hoping that this was the right thing to do. Though I was trying to believe what they were saying was true, it was hard. Boy, did I miss Veida. With her I didn't have to worry about none of that. Maybe all four of us could be friends. Was I getting soft or what?

It wasn't until Tuesday of the next week that Veida came back to school. I rushed up to her and stood there with my hands on my hips, waiting for an explanation.

"Girl, I missed you . . ." she said to me.

And then when I got the feeling that everything was okay, I tapped her lightly on her side with my purse. "Why haven't you called me? You know I've been worried. I left several messages. Where have you been?"

"Can't you tell by my voice?"

As I listened to her talk some more, I could tell that she did sound a little hoarse.

"Yeah, were you sick or something? You were absent for six days."

"I was in the hospital. I got my tonsils out."

Shocked, I replied, "You were in the hospital and I didn't know?"

"Yeah, 'cause I was in the hospital *and* on punishment."

"How can you be on punishment in the hospital?" I asked her.

"I had an eight-hundred-dollar cell phone bill."

"Are you serious? You and I talk all the time, but we don't talk *that* much."

Veida shared, "My dad was livid."

"I've heard of big phone bills, but eight hundred dollars worth? Veida . . . what's up?"

"I was talking to my old friends. It's not my fault that my

parents moved me away from them. I had to text them all the time, and that stuff adds up."

"I didn't even know you were going to have your tonsils out. I was praying for you, girl. I could've been there for you."

"I know. Again, my dad was mad. I'm still on punishment too. I don't even want to be around him because he's so upset with me. He says I have no respect for money. I know that's a lot of money and I plan to work it off some way, somehow. I just don't know how he expects me to live without my cell phone now. How am I supposed to talk to my friends?"

Part of me was a little jealous; I didn't know that she was still hanging on to old friendships from her past. I already had to share her with my brother. Now I had to share her with her old friends too. *Maybe the no-phone thing wouldn't be so bad,* I thought. She and I could talk to each other more.

"What are you thinking about?" she asked.

"Mmm . . . nothing."

"No, you're thinking about something. Tell me, I see that silly look on your face. Explain."

I said, "I really don't know. It's just that I didn't know you were still talking to your old friends."

"Aww . . . somebody is jealous," she said playfully.

"No, I'm not. I just didn't know," I uttered as I scratched my head.

"Yeah, I'm still cool with some of my old friends. Of course I told them about you and your brother. No one thought I was going to like this school—not even me. But I wouldn't move back even if they paid my eight-hundred-dollar cell phone bill. Okay, well maybe I would move back for that."

We both laughed.

"Yeah, girl, you're my best friend. It killed me not being able to talk to you. But I wrote you lots of letters. Here," Veida said.

She went into her book bag and pulled out eight letters in the prettiest pastel envelopes I'd ever seen.

"I didn't want you to find another best friend while I was gone, so to show you I care about you, I wrote all my thoughts down."

Before I could grab the letters, Asia and Perlicia walked up and came between us.

"Hey, girl," Asia said, hugging me real tight. "Ooh . . . what's this?" she said, looking at the letters and then grabbing some of them.

"They're mine!" I said, quickly yanking them out of her hands.

Veida said angrily, "You know they don't belong to you. They're for my friend."

"Well, she's *our* friend now, and no secrets," Asia said as she opened the one envelope she had managed to hold on to.

"How dare you open my stuff!" I said indignantly.

Perlicia said, "Well, if we're friends we share stuff, right?"

"She's friends with y'all. Huh, I don't think so," Veida said, looking at me for an explanation.

I uttered, "It's a long, long story."

"So listen," Asia said to me as she stood in front of Veida, "we're fine now with you liking Myrek."

"I never said I liked Myrek."

"Yes, you did. When we were with him in the hall you said you liked him," Asia reminded me.

"What?" Veida said, smiling.

I hesitantly admitted, "Okay, well maybe I did say I liked him, but I wasn't serious."

"Yes, you were," Perlicia said to me. "Since you have two brothers, we figure one can be for Asia and one can be for me. We can all go on a date together to the Fall Ball on Friday."

"York doesn't like to get dressed up for that kind of stuff," I said.

"And Yancy," Veida starting to roll her neck, cut in and said, "wouldn't want to gò with either one of you guys."

"First of all, nobody is talking to you," Asia said as she put her hand in Veida's face.

"You goody-two-shoes rich girl, please get out of my face," Perlicia said to her.

"Y'all need to chill," I said.

I had to pull them away from each other. I didn't want us to have tension. Knowing they were talking about getting with Yancy wasn't sitting well with Veida.

"We'll see y'all later," I said to Perlicia and Asia as I pushed Veida down the hall.

"You really want to be friends with them?" Veida asked me.

"They're not really my kind, so I wouldn't go out of my way to be with them, but maybe we can just be associates and get along. My mom says you have friends and then you have people you know that you can be cool with from a distance. You know what I mean?"

"Yeah, I guess, but it still seems that they are just using you so they can hook up with your brothers," Veida said with passion. "Can't you see that? They don't really want to be your friends!"

"You like one of my brothers!" I retorted.

She stopped walking. "Yasmin, I do need something bad."

"What? What do you mean?" I asked.

"I want to spend the night. I want to spend some time with Yancy, and you know my dad won't have that. So we have to make him think your brothers won't be there."

I told her, "My mom is not going to let you spend the night at my house. She knows my brother likes you. No way."

"So, just like that you won't even try to make it happen."

"I know you not gonna get mad at me because I told you I'm not going to do it. Right? You said you wrote all these letters to let me know how much of a friend I am to you. Now you get an attitude because I won't do what you want. Trust me when I say that you don't want to go too fast with any guy and chase after him, whether it's my brother or not."

"I just know that friends go out of their way for each other, Yasmin. And if you're not willing to do that for me, then I don't know what kind of friendship we have."

"Then I don't know either," I said to her, lifting my hands. But I did know that I wasn't willing to compromise my integrity.

I didn't want a best friend that would get mad at me because I wouldn't grant her every demand. Whatever our friendship was going to be, it would be. She went her way, and I went mine.

"Why are you sittin' here like a bump on a log?" Myrek said to me as I sat on the bleachers alone.

Actually, I didn't want to be at the Fall Ball. The week had ended so crazy. Just as I'd thought in the beginning, Asia and Perlicia proved that they didn't really want to be my friends. When I wouldn't set them up with my brothers or Myrek, they tossed me away quicker than trash. Of course, I could deal with not having them as friends.

What really got to me was my troubled relationship with Veida. I thought that she and I were going to be buddies. But she really was upset with me that I wouldn't go for her sleeping over at my house. So instead of arguing about it, we just stayed away from each other. I wasn't a whiner or a complainer. I didn't want to talk negatively about someone I cared about and had issues with. So I chose not to talk to anybody, including Myrek, even though I knew he had my back. I just kept my distance from everyone.

When the only other option was to stay home and be even more bored, I decided to go to the Fall Ball with my brothers. However, as expected, as soon as we stepped in the place, Yancy was gone with Veida. Then York got in the car with some high school guys and left the scene.

"Oh, so you not even gon' talk to me?" Myrek said, sitting beside me without an invitation.

I wondered why people did that. Why was it when I was alone that people thought I wanted company? Did I have *please come and spend time with me* written all over my face?

"Look, don't be mad at me. I just wanted to see if you'd like to dance. If I'm bugging you, annoying you, or whatever, I'll leave you alone," Myrek said as I just sat there not responding.

I just gave Myrek a blank look; he got up and just stood there looking at me. But before he could walk away, I felt I should explain myself so that his feelings wouldn't be hurt.

I said, "Hey, I'm not mad at you. I'm just stressed."

"Stressed about what?"

"I don't know. It just seems like things are going wrong. I can't explain it. I have no control over what people do. It just makes me crazy."

"Well, you've got to stop worrying about other people and have some fun, Yas."

"Yeah, that's easy to say."

Then a fun song came on. "It's the electric slide, Yasmin. Come on, girl. I know you want to hit the floor. You know that's your song!" Myrek grinned at me.

"Okay, let's go," I said.

We went to the dance floor and I put the first smile on my face I'd had in a long time. Dipping down, getting up, kicking, moving to the left and the right was a bunch of fun. Being out there with Myrek was special. Like he said, I had to quit letting what people said or did get me down. Of course that was easier said than done. As soon as Myrek and I left the dance floor, Veida ran up to me with Yancy following behind her.

She said, "Okay, I know we haven't talked in a while—"

"How about for a week?" I said interrupting.

Yancy looked at Myrek. "Hey, let the ladies talk; we can go and get them some punch or something."

Myrek responded, "Cool. Yasmin, you want something to drink?"

"Yes, please," I said to him before he walked away with Yancy. "Well, now that my brother has given us time to talk, what is it? You're not coming over to my house to spend the night, Veida. It's just not going to happen."

"That's cool, that's cool. Well, see what I need is . . ." She hushed up when a chaperone approached us.

"You ladies having a good time?" the assistant principal asked.

"Yeah, we're having a ball," Veida responded with a fake smile.

As he walked away, I yanked at her sweater to pull her closer to me. "What's going on? What do you need?"

"See, I've scouted out all of the chaperones. And when the music begins, they start looking at the dance floor. You know a lot of kids are dancing a little too close. So they have to go and break them apart."

"Uh-huh, what about it?" I asked.

"Well, when the next song starts, your brother and I are going under."

"Under where?" I asked.

"Shhhh," she said to me as she pointed under the bleachers.

"And what do you want me to do?"

"Look out for a sister and your brother. Just stomp when you see a chaperone coming. We'll move away from each other and everything will be fine."

"I'm not going to be your lookout person, Veida."

"Yes, you've got to do it. Yancy and I want some time together. You don't want me to come over to your house. Yasmin, why are you making such a big deal out of this?"

"Why are you going under the bleachers with my brother? Guys are supposed to chase us. Don't make it easy for him. I'm making a big deal out of it because if that's what you want to do then don't include me!"

"Nothing's gonna happen. Quit worrying."

"I'm not worrying. I'm not the one trying to do something wrong."

"Well, thank you for the sermon—but just be on the lookout."

Yancy came back without Myrek. Yancy and Veida couldn't

stop staring each other down. He thanked me before I got a chance to tell him I wouldn't have his back. For two songs I just sat there. I wasn't really watching out for them, I just wasn't out on the floor dancing.

Then I started thinking. I didn't know where Myrek was. But just as I was sitting there, feeling like I was sort of helping them, Myrek rushed over to me. He was spilling punch everywhere.

"What's going on?" I stood up to keep from getting splashed.

"Come here," he called out and motioned.

"I can't leave."

"No, this is important. Come here. You've got to be able to hear."

I rushed over to him. Why was it always something? Myrek's stressed face said something wasn't right.

When Myrek handed me his cell phone, I said, "Hello?"

Then York's frantic voice jumped through the phone. "Sis, this is serious. I had to call you on Myrek's phone because I need you to get Ma."

"What are you talking about, York?"

"I'm in jail."

"What?"

"They took me to juvey."

"I don't understand. What did you do?" I asked, hoping this was a misunderstanding.

"I took a couple of things at the mall."

"York, you *stole* some stuff? How stupid is that?"

"Look, I don't have no time for a lecture, and I don't have a lot of time period. I need you to get Ma. I tried but I couldn't get her. Then y'all need to come get me. I don't want to be locked up all night."

As soon as I turned around, I saw Mr. Caldwell, our principal, and a teacher escorting Yancy and Veida from underneath the bleachers. I'd left my post. All of this just couldn't be happening.

I turned to the other stable person I knew. "Myrek, I told you this night is crazy. You said not to stress, not to let any of it get to me, but my life is all a mess. One brother is going to the principal's office, the other is in jail . . . this is a mess." I knew I wasn't a worrier by default.

Chapter 7

Observer of Drama

"Myrek, did you just see that?" I screamed out, pacing back and forth.

Trying to get me to stop moving, Myrek said, "Yeah, yeah, calm down."

"Calm down?" I challenged, like he had to be kidding. "Mr. Caldwell and another teacher just caught my brother and Veida!"

"Well, what did York want?" he asked me.

"He's in jail!"

"What? He sounded like it was serious, but man!"

"Yeah, shoplifting!"

"I told that boy he was cool enough with those clothes," Myrek said as he took a seat on the bleachers. It seemed like all that was going on was even too much for him.

"My mom is going to trip. With everything else going on, now she's gonna have to deal with the principal and the police. I need to call her."

"Sure," he said handing me his cell phone.

When I dialed my mom's number, Veida walked past me rolling her eyes as a female teacher escorted her out of the gym. I knew she was upset that I let her down. I knew she was thinking that I was supposed to be watching. But, it wasn't my fault. I had to take York's phone call. Besides, I never agreed to watch out for them anyway. Maybe I should have told them that I had to take the phone, but it all happened so quickly. This is just proof that when you do wrong, it doesn't work out right.

I had no idea that Mom's cell phone had been disconnected. I knew she barely had money to give us for the dance. Now I was wondering how I was going to get in touch with her.

Kicking the bleacher, I said, "I can't get my mom."

"Is it going straight to voice mail?"

"No, it's disconnected."

"Well, just call her job."

"I don't know the number."

"You know where she works," he said pointing to my head. "Just call information."

"She doesn't like for us to call her job."

"This is a double emergency. She'll understand."

Taking Myrek's advice, I called information for the number to my mom's job. She worked on the janitorial staff at this place called The Landing. It was an exclusive indoor-outdoor mall off the riverfront in downtown Jacksonville.

"Hello?" an unfamiliar voice answered.

"Yes, I'm calling to speak to Yvette Peace, please."

"I'm sorry, she's working right now. I can take a message for her."

"Please, I've got to speak to my mother right now, it's an emergency!"

"Okay, okay. Hold on . . . let me get the supervisor."

As I waited, I got up and continued to pace back and forth. Still on hold five minutes later, I sat down. This was too much to bear.

Myrek said, "Okay, what's takin' them so long? You still on hold?"

I nodded. "She's going to get the supervisor. At first she told me that I might not be able to talk to her."

When I finally spoke to the supervisor, I was very nervous. However, after I explained everything to her, she agreed to promptly locate my mom. After about five more minutes, my mother was on the line.

"Yasmin Peace, this better be something good. I can't believe you're calling me at work. You know this lady don't want me takin' no calls. I told you I couldn't get off to take y'all home. So if Myrek's dad can't pick you up, then y'all just gon' have to walk."

"No, Ma, no. That's not what I'm calling for," I said after finally getting a word in.

"What's goin' on then?"

"It's the boys, Ma."

Changing her irritated voice to a panicked one, she asked, "What, what happened to the boys? They haven't been in no accident have they?"

It amazed me that she went from being severely mad to being severely worried. I only wished I didn't have to give her the bad news about them.

"What's going on, Yasmin?" she asked when I wasn't speaking quickly enough.

"York is in jail."

"In jail?"

"Yeah, he left the dance and went to the mall with some high school dudes from our neighborhood. He stole something and got caught. He said you can call Duval County Jail and they'll give you the details."

After taking a deep breath, she asked, "And what about Yancy? He left the dance too?"

"No ma'am. He got caught under the bleachers."

"What was he doing under the bleachers?"

"He was . . . with a girl."

My mom's anger returned. "I told that boy . . . was it Veida?"

"Yeah, and you've got to come now because he's in the principal's office."

"I can't believe this. I have to leave my job. I'm gonna get fired for having too many distractions. I don't know what's wrong with y'all. Bye!"

I stood there with tears rolling down my face. Why did she have to include me with York and Yancy? I wasn't trying to be the model child or anything, but I didn't know why my mother had to be so upset with me when I didn't do anything wrong. Yeah, I was the bearer of bad news, but I didn't do it myself. Why did she have to go off on me? Myrek just came over and gave me a hug. I appreciated his friendship more than he knew.

He and I waited in the lobby for my mom. When she pulled up, her eyes looked like someone had socked her in them. I could tell she had been crying the whole way to the school.

As one of the chaperones opened the door for her, I rushed up to her and said, "Ma, I'm sorry."

"I'm sorry too, Yasmin. I know you think I'm mad at you but I'm not. This is just really hard. Taking it out on you wasn't my intention. It's just that as hard as I try with you kids, it just keeps going wrong. Jeff's gone, York's in jail, Yancy's in trouble, and I might get fired. And to make things even worse, it don't help that y'all's daddy is locked up too. Why are so many things going wrong for this family? Lord, help me," she said before we walked into the school hallway.

When we got to the office, Myrek and I sat outside.

The principal, Mr. Caldwell, came out and said to my mom, "Mrs. Peace, I'm glad you're here. We have a serious problem on our hands. Please come in."

Myrek and I couldn't wait to find out what was going on, but we would have to depend on Yancy to tell us what happened. We knew that Mr. Caldwell would say that there were rules at our school that must be abided by during school hours as well as after school hours.

Yancy had never been suspended or even had a detention for that matter. Except for his grades falling off recently, he'd been a model student. Veida was new to the school and hadn't been in trouble either, although I didn't know if she had a bad record from her previous school.

"Veida, you don't let some boy influence you to do something you shouldn't be doing!" We heard Veida's dad, Mr. Hatchett, say as they exited Mr. Caldwell's office.

Mom interrupted, "Okay now, who says that my son was the one doin' the influencing here? He said that he simply kissed your daughter and even that was not forced. You need to tell her not to be so fast and chase after boys. And another thing, I don't know what Veida told you, but Yasmin never asked me about her spending the night. Plus, I would never allow that, knowing she and Yancy like each other."

Mr. Hatchett turned to his daughter and scolded her. "Young lady, you know I would never let you sleep over Yasmin's house if I knew she had two brothers your age. I don't know and don't care what other parents allow their kids to do," he said as he looked Myrek up and down, "but you can't do what everybody else does."

"Stop allowing people to influence you, Veida. You told me that Yasmin invited you to stay over sometimes. So that's what this is all about, you being interested in her brother. You were trying to be slick, huh?"

Veida didn't open her mouth.

My mom had borrowed Myrek's cell phone to call his dad, so she didn't hear what Mr. Hatchett had said about me influencing Veida. If she would've heard that, we would've never gotten out of the parking lot.

I whispered to Veida, "If you cared about me and Yancy, you would open up your mouth and tell your dad that you invited yourself over to spend the night and that I wouldn't go along with it. You need to tell him that you were the one who approached me with your little scheme to go under the bleachers with Yancy. You are no better than Asia and Perlicia," I said in the meanest tone I could muster.

As she got into her car, tears started streaming down her face. I couldn't have cared less. She could have cried enough to make a new river and I wouldn't have felt sorry for her.

When we got into our car, my mom said to Yancy, "Now, you and Veida are suspended for four days all because you did something you knew you weren't supposed to do. Son, you'd better leave them fast girls alone! The only thing you should've been doing with that girl was dancing!"

It was good to know that Yancy wasn't in trouble by himself. It was just too bad that Veida's dad still thought that Yancy and I were bad influences.

Just then Myrek's dad pulled up to get him and we all said good-bye.

Now that we'd gotten past this incident, it seemed like Mom was a bit calmer. But since we were on our way to get York—it wouldn't be long before she'd be boiling over again.

~❧~

I couldn't believe we were pulling up to the Duval County Jail. I had never been there before and knew I'd never want to return.

York was a hothead, but he was a good kid. What made him move to stealing was way beyond me. But if it turned out to be clothes that he stole, I wouldn't be surprised.

My mom went up to the counter and said, "I'm here to get my baby. It's late. Y'all need to let him out. His name is York Peace. I need to speak to someone that can get my baby out right now, right now!"

"Ma'am, hold on now," an officer said to her. "You have to fill out some papers and then have a seat."

"Aww, somebody gon' let him out tonight!" The officer could see this was a mom with nothing to lose.

"Let me go and get someone to talk to you who's over your son's case."

I went over to my mom and said, "Ma, you've got to calm down."

"Yasmin, we are at a police station and it's 10:30 at night. Plus, I should still be at work. Do you think I look like someone who cares to look calm? I'm tryin' to get my son out of here, and he better not be up in here with no adult men."

It was the longest ten minutes in my lifetime. My mother wore out the rubber on the bottom of her work shoes pacing, as she waited on someone to give her some direction.

Just as she sat down to rest her feet, someone walked up and said, "Ma'am, I'm Officer Floyd, the juvenile officer. I understand you're Peace's mom. I need to go over this paperwork with you regarding a hearing for your son and then I can release him into your custody."

"Okay—but where is he?" my mom said, looking relieved.

"Follow me," he answered.

She stood to her feet. "My son has never been arrested in his life. Do I have to pay to get him out, or what?"

"No, ma'am. He'll get a date for a hearing and at that time you'll pay whatever fines there are."

Hearing that made me remember about the modeling opportunity I had. That would give me money to help Mom pay York's fine. I needed to think about calling that lady to sign up.

Yancy and I were told to wait while Mom went with the officer.

My brother interrupted my thoughts by saying, "I'm in trouble, but York . . . oohh weee! He might have to move down with Uncle John."

"You're the only one that wants to leave. Hopefully neither one of you won't have to do that and cause Ma all that grief. I still can't believe you and Veida," I scolded.

Yancy responded, "I can handle Ma. Being out of school a few days is no big deal. I care about the girl, all right? You're just jealous that you don't have a dad who is there like hers and that your dad's locked up," he continued.

"What are you trying to say, Yancy? He's your daddy too."

"Yeah, don't remind me. I'm just playing with you, girl."

"Whatever, Yancy."

"Yeah, whatever."

Just then, Mom came out with York. The tough look he normally had on his face was gone. I got up and hugged him. He said, "I'm sorry, y'all. I'm sorry."

My two brothers just looked at each other and didn't say a word.

"Let's just go home. I have to be at work early in the morning," my mom said in a deflated voice.

We all got into the car to head home. No one said a word. Then all of a sudden, Mom was about to run a red light.

York yelled out, "Yo, Ma, STOP!"

She slammed on the brakes. All of us fell forward and then jerked back real hard.

"I've got to pull over, I can't do this. I'm trying so hard, Lord. Now I don't have rent money. I lost money for gettin' off early and I'm gonna lose money to take off for York's hearing date. Lord, what am I going to do? One son was arrested, the other son suspended. I can't take this. I just can't. I've lost one of my babies. Can't You help me with the others?"

She pulled over, got out of the car, and walked to the side. Then she hit the car several times and just cried. None of us said anything. I didn't know whether to get out and console her or what. After a few moments, she wiped her tears and got back in the car.

"It's all right, y'all. I'm okay. It's tight and I don't know how we gon' make it to the end of this month, but we gon' make it. I hope things will turn around because I don't like being in or an observer of drama."

Chapter 8

Madder
Each Moment

"Ma! Get up!" I was getting a little irritated that my mom kept ignoring me.

It seemed like I'd called her fifty times already. Mondays were her day to clean at the hospital. Normally she would be waking up early for work but today was different.

The past week had been rough on our family, with Yancy being on in-school suspension and York waiting on his juvenile hearing. And today was the day that York would find out his punishment at the hearing.

I understood why my mom slept in on Saturday and Sunday, although I had hoped that we could have gone to church on Sunday the way we used to a few years back. Every time one of us came in to check on her, she had complained about a headache. I hated to admit it, but she was severely depressed. Maybe she needed to do like I did and talk to a counselor or something. Even York and Yancy probably needed to do that too.

Being a little salty with my brothers, I quickly went into their room, slammed the door, and turned on the light.

I yelled, "It's time to get up, y'all."

"It's too early," York said, throwing his pillow toward the door where I stood.

I caught it and threw it back at him, making sure it rammed him in the head. "Get up!"

"Give me a few more minutes," Yancy said as he pulled the covers over his head.

"Me too," York echoed. "Now turn off the light and close the door!"

"Guys, you don't understand. We need to find a way to get Ma out of her depressed mood."

They both sat up. It was the first time I had actually gone in and sat on the empty bed in their room. I hated the fact that Jeff wasn't here to help me set the two of them straight.

I prayed, *Help me, Lord. My brothers are looking at me like I'm buggin'. Why do they think I'm not making any sense? Lord, please help me with the words to make my brothers understand that they need to get their acts together.*

"What do you want us to do?" York said, getting my attention back.

"I guess I want you to care. I mean, it's like . . . York, you risked stealing to wear new clothes. Yancy, you risked getting suspended from school with Veida. How are y'all willing to go out of your way for Ma?"

All I heard was silence. When it didn't seem to matter to them, I started to leave. Then Yancy pulled me back into the room by saying, "She's right, York. We've got to do better."

"It's all this stuff y'all are putting her through. She can't take it. I know it will help her feel better if she gets good news at your hearing today," I said to York.

"Yeah, you're right, Yas."

"And Yancy, if you get your focus back on your books instead of on girls, Ma will be happy about that," I said.

"Yeah, I know," Yancy said, looking at me with a dejected glare.

Shortly after I left their room, Yancy and I had to get dressed for school. When we opened the door to leave, York came out of the room and stopped us.

"Take care of Ma, York," Yancy said.

"I will, man."

"York, I prayed for you and your hearing today. I know you might not think that helps, but it does," I added.

"Thanks, Yas."

Yancy and I started running to the bus stop when it looked like we were about to miss the bus. Thankfully, the driver saw us. When we got on the bus, I went to an empty seat and plopped down.

"Hey, Yasmin, you can't speak?" Myrek said in an agitated tone.

I gave him a half wave and a fake smile. I saw him sitting there before I sat down. I wasn't trying to be rude, but my family was in a crisis. It wasn't time to be social. I didn't have time to chitchat with him. All of my thoughts were put into how I could get my mom out of her depression.

❧

Of course, the first person that I saw when I went to my locker was Veida.

"Okay, all right, Yasmin. I know you're mad at me," Veida came up to me and said. "But you know what? You're not too high up on my list of girlfriends either."

"I don't care!" I said, waiting for her to bring it.

"You know how my dad is. I couldn't tell him that I was the one who asked you to be a lookout for me and Yancy or that I was trying to spend the night at your house."

I could have socked her. Then, if my morning hadn't started badly enough, Asia and Perlicia—the two little busybodies or flies on the walls—had been nearby listening the whole time. I wanted to punch them too. I sure needed the Lord to calm me down quick.

Perlicia said, "I told you she wasn't really your friend, Yasmin. You were worried about us getting with your brothers. At least we wouldn't have dogged them out."

Veida said, "You guys need to mind your own business. Neither York nor Yancy is interested in the two of you."

Placing my hand in their faces, I uttered, "You know what, guys, I don't need to hear any of this. I don't trust her," pointing to Veida, "and I definitely don't trust you all either."

"Ugh! I can't even believe you would say that," Perlicia said.

"Let's go," Asia told her.

Good riddance! I thought as I saw the backs of their heads.

Veida started at me, "You know, this is all your fault. None of us would have had to go through any of this if you had just done what I asked you to do. You've got the nerve to be mad at me, Yasmin. There is no need for me to take the blame for something I had already worked out."

Then she turned around and tried to walk away without me getting in a word.

I followed her and said, "If you want to talk to me, Veida, we can do that, but you need to be real in hearing me out too."

"What, Yasmin? What you got to say? If only you could have been the lookout. Why couldn't you just stand there and watch for me, even if you didn't agree?"

"I was standing there, but then I got an emergency call from York. He got arrested for stealing from the mall. A few seconds of not being a watchdog for you was enough for the principal to walk by. I didn't want to be responsible for that anyway and I never said I would. You had your dad thinking that I was the one influencing you to stay at my house when I told you over and over again that I didn't want you to be there. If we call ourselves speaking from the heart, then what's up with that?"

"Yasmin, I'm just seeing things differently and maybe it's best for us to go our separate ways," Veida responded.

"Yeah, maybe it is."

However, when we started going in separate directions, a part of me wanted to reconcile and get it all out. I know girls get older and change, but I was so angry with her for wanting to be too fast. Anyway, who knows, maybe I would fall for a guy that way someday. I hoped not ever though.

She was so into my brother that she had started lying. Having her dad think that I was the one trying to get her to spend the night at my house was not cool. That was way out of left field and a person that was going to tell lies on me most certainly wasn't my friend. And even though I would miss her, cutting that connection was probably best.

When we got home from school, York was all smiles.

"I'm not in trouble, y'all!" York said, slapping hands with Yancy. I was so happy to hear some good news.

"What's up, man? What happened?" Yancy asked excitedly.

"I just talked to the judge and explained to him the situation and everything we had been going through. I said I was sorry and that I knew I was wrong. They gave me community service. I have to work on a neighborhood cleaning project."

"Don't be bragging, boy. They gon' keep that money that I gave them for your stupid mistake. We don't even have rent money. This ain't the greatest situation," Mom yelled. "You kids just don't understand. Yeah, Yancy, you're not suspended, but you have an in-school suspension. It's still gon' be on your record. Those teachers who thought you were a model student are now going to think twice. And, York, your stuff is not over!"

York said, "But they said it wouldn't be on my record."

"Look, smartie," she said, coming over and swatting him with a newspaper, "you've still got community service. And who do you think has to take off work to get your behind there? I lost money taking you today too. I gotta make up that money somehow. All of this taking off work, I'll probably lose that job! And, Yasmin—"

I hadn't done anything wrong at the party. I hadn't gotten into any trouble with the law. I had pretty good grades. Now that York's situation was sort of settled and Yancy completed his in-school suspension, I thought maybe things were improving a little. But if she lost her job, what were we going to do?

She motioned for me to come to our bedroom door. "I asked you not to go to bed with the kitchen looking a mess, and even though I was sick all weekend, it's like you didn't pick up a thing. Did you clean the bathroom? Did you wash any clothes? . . . just so lazy, makes me crazy. I've got to work and then come home to clean up. Must I do it all myself? Could you help? All y'all just make me sick."

"But, Ma—" I didn't even get a chance to tell her who the culprits were because she stormed into the bedroom.

"She's still mad at us," York said after she shut the door, leaving us to ponder her words.

"Yeah, but I guess we deserve it," Yancy said.

"You two deserve it. You both know I cleaned up all weekend. You guys don't pick up after yourselves. Because she's in a foul mood I get blamed for everything. Honestly, I'm mad too!" I said as they mocked me by making sad faces.

❧

The next day at school, I didn't want to sit in the counselor's office and pour my heart out anymore. I mean, what could she tell me that could help? I was trying to stand on my faith by surrendering everything to the Lord. However, every time I let Him take the lead in my life, things seemed to get worse.

"You really don't want to know how I'm doing, so please don't ask me," I said to Mrs. Newman. I was having a pity party.

"Well, I called you in here because I saw you in the hallway earlier trying to open your locker. You were kicking it and hitting it. What's wrong?"

She wanted to play the nice card by telling me she understood me. How could she understand when I didn't even get what was going on? I just sat there for a minute and twiddled my thumbs. I wasn't ready to go back to class. I did have stuff inside of me that I wanted to get out. I needed advice more than I needed lunch in another couple of minutes.

"Why does it seem like God doesn't care about me?" I asked her.

"What do you mean? What makes you say that?" Mrs. Newman asked.

"It's bad enough that we're poor and we can barely make it. But now it seems worse. My mom doesn't know how she's going to get dinner from one day to the next. And she might even lose one of her jobs because she had to go to a hearing for one of my brothers. Besides, my other brother got an in-school suspension. Even when I try to do everything right to please her so she won't get mad at me, it backfires. It's like she hates me or doesn't see that I'm trying. If God loved me, He would see that I can't take all of this. So I'm asking you, why doesn't the Lord show that He loves me?"

"He does love you. Sure you're having a tough time right now. It may seem that you have it harder than many others do, and you just might. But there are a lot of kids that have single moms trying to make ends meet without a dad in their homes."

"But all my issues hit at the same time. He even gave me a friend and then took her away. I finally got a new perm in my hair, and I don't have enough money to keep that up. It isn't right."

"Are you praying?"

"I pray all of the time, but it seems that He doesn't hear me."

"My grandmother told me when I was your age that He may not come when you want Him, but He'll be there right on time," Mrs. Newman offered.

"What does that mean? I need Him now and He's not here now."

"Just because it doesn't seem like He's there working it out, or just because your feelings get the best of you doesn't mean that He doesn't love or care for you. It doesn't mean that He's not on your side. Yasmin, I want to be honest with you. I can't tell you why He does this and why He does that. However, I know He has never left me. My life hasn't been a bed of roses either. I've had some pretty rough days, but through it all, I trust Him. He hears our prayers and He answers them. He just may not answer the way we want."

Then she opened up her desk drawer and pulled out a very cute pink Bible that looked like a magazine and said, "I get into this. Here, take it."

"I wouldn't know where to begin," I said.

"This is just the New Testament. Start at the beginning. But before you start reading, ask the Lord to give you understanding. He will. He loves you, Yasmin. Through all of this He is making you stronger; He's making you better. He just wants you to love Him more, and He wants you to bring it all to Him. Even when you're bummed out, He's God and He can take it. At your darkest hour you need to turn to Him for light. And this might surprise you, but I see God clearly working in your life."

"I don't see it, Mrs. Newman."

"Yasmin, the fact that you're here in my office pouring out your concerns for family members that you love shows that the love of God is in your heart. It's true that you might not know what the answers are or what to do about all of the problems, but the best thing is that you're talking with me, and I'm directing you to give it all to Him. Does that make sense?"

"Yeah, I think it does," I said as I stood up and gave her a hug.

⊰◈⊱

Later that day, I finished my homework and went outside. I needed to get some exercise, but I wasn't trying to walk through the neighborhood and run into Bone and his crew. I certainly didn't want to see them. However, I did need to do something so I stayed on my street and walked back and forth. I looked over my shoulder and saw Myrek coming toward me with a basketball. I was exercising so I didn't want to stop and hold a conversation. As soon as he came closer, I simply waved and kept moving.

He yelled out, "Hey, what's going on with that? You didn't speak to me on the bus. Actually, you haven't spoken to me in awhile. Are you mad at me or something?"

"No, I saw you with your basketball and you need to start practicing. I need to stay in shape too, so I just said hi. I mean, what else did you want me to say?"

"Can I just be honest and break it down to you?" Myrek asked.

"Yeah sure, what?"

"I like you and you told me that you liked me. We live right next door to each other, but if it weren't for us riding the bus together, I would never see you. Why don't you be my girlfriend?"

If I had been drinking something I probably would have spit it out and choked. I did manage to laugh in his face; however, that wasn't the response he wanted. But I couldn't help it. I wasn't ready to be anybody's girlfriend. I mean, yeah, he was cool, but even all of that was weirding me out. Couldn't he just understand that I had pulled away for a reason?

"Why you gon' laugh like that? If you don't wanna be with me then that's all you have to say. There are plenty of girls trying to get with me. I don't need you anyway, Yasmin."

Before I had a chance to apologize, he dribbled away at full speed. I didn't want to be his girlfriend, but I did care about him.

I just hoped that Mrs. Newman was right because no matter what I did, stuff was getting messed up. People I cared about were practically done with me—seemingly getting madder each moment.

Chapter 9

Wiser through Visiting

I was so glad it was Thanksgiving vacation so we could have family time. Also, I needed a break from school. We were riding down the highway on our way to see my grandmother in Orlando. I was really disappointed when we didn't make it down there last Thanksgiving. And I know my mom didn't want to go as bad as us kids did, but she did say that maybe getting away from our surroundings might help. For me, it was all about seeing Big Mama. She always knew just the right words to say.

"Now when folks ask us how we're doing, I don't want to see no tears and no pity parties. We didn't come here lookin' for hand-outs. We'll make it without folks all in our business! Do y'all hear me?" My mother was schooling us as we pulled into her mother's driveway after the exhausting ride.

"Yes, ma'am," we said in unison.

Big Mama was standing on her front porch waiting for our arrival.

As we exited the car, she stood there with her arms stretched wide, waiting to give us all big bear hugs. "Yasmin, you look so pretty," she told me. It felt so good to be in her arms again.

"And look at these handsome young men here," she said smiling and hugging them both. Mom and Big Mama then embraced one another with an extended hug. It made me smile to see my mom wrapped in her mother's arms.

After all the hugging, York asked the next logical question, which I'm sure Yancy wanted the answer to as well.

"Big Mama, you got some fried chicken? I know I smell somethin' good."

"Boy, we just stopped and got you a hamburger. You can't be that hungry," Mom said, shaking her head.

"York, now you know I wouldna been expecting y'all and not have some food ready. Even though tomorrow is Thanksgiving, I had to fix a little somethin' for y'all getting here today. I've got fried chicken, catfish, cornbread, spaghetti, cold slaw, and peach cobbler. Your Aunt Yolonda and your cousins will be over tomorrow and we'll have a big ol' feast like always! Yasmin, would you help your ol' grandma make the sweet potato pies tonight?"

"Oh, yes ma'am!" I said in anticipation.

"All this talk about food is makin' me even more hungry. I'm ready to eat," York said, licking his lips.

"All of that does sound good, Ma," my mother said with a smile on her face.

"Y'all come on in and freshen up and we'll get started. Yasmin, you can help me set the table," she said as she winked at me.

After we set the table, we blessed the food and everybody began to dig in. "So, what's goin' on with y'all?" Big Mama asked.

Everybody just looked around the table at each other and then my mom said, "Ma, we're good."

"Hmm . . . don't look like it to me, Yvette."

"Ma, please. We makin' it. Ain't nothin' perfect," my mother said obviously irritated.

Big Mama looked at all of us kids closer. I could tell she was just waiting for us to bust out and say something to contradict what Mom said, but we kept eating and acted like we were in another world.

York was the first to break our silence. "Big Mama, we might be going to see Daddy."

My mom had mentioned to us on the drive down that we might be going to visit Dad in jail.

Then Yancy said, "Well, I want to see Uncle John."

York wanted to see Dad, and Yancy wanted to see our uncle. And I wasn't sure what I wanted.

"I told y'all that I would think about it and see. I don't know what we're gonna do. Right now I don't wanna think about seein' nobody," my mother said emphatically.

"Now, just calm down, ain't nothin' wrong with these boys wantin' some male influence around," Big Mama said.

"I know, Ma, but they need the right influence. I'm not sure if takin' them to a jail is the best thing to do right now."

"Ma, I don't want to see Daddy," Yancy said quickly.

"And I don't wanna see Uncle John," York shot back.

"Why do you want to see Daddy anyway? What has he really done for you?" Yancy asked.

York said, "At least I want to see my real dad. You still livin' in a fantasy world like Uncle John is your father. You always trying to act like you got more than you do."

Yancy replied, "Whatever. I'm not the one getting caught in the mall stealing clothes. I'm perfectly happy with the ones I have."

"Do I need to whup both of y'all?" my mother said.

Big Mama jumped in. "They're almost getting too ol' for that, Yvette."

"Ma, I can handle this," my mom said.

Big Mama continued, "I'm just saying, let those boys talk like men. If your father was—"

My mom cut her off. "Ma, my father ain't here. He's dead, okay? I'm not a perfect parent like the two of you were. I'm sorry that I married a drug dealer who's doin' time and left me with four kids. I'm holdin' it down the best I can. I love them with my whole heart, and I don't need you criticizing me."

"But, baby that's just it. I'm not criticizing you. I'm just saying you should take some help," Big Mama said in a sweet tone. Seems like she was encouraging my mom to do what I'd been doing. Going to see my counselor at school was my way of getting help and encouragement.

"Ma, I just want to see Daddy," York said.

"And I just want to talk to Uncle John," Yancy added.

Mom said, "York, you think your dad can do no wrong. And, Yancy, you already told me that you wanted to live with your uncle. I can't lose you two. I'm the parent here."

"We know that, Ma," Yancy said as he bent over to give her a kiss.

"Yeah, Ma, we ain't goin' nowhere," York said as he stroked her back.

"Okay, we're all goin' to see y'all's daddy," my mom said seemingly overwhelmed.

Big Mama said, "That's a wise decision, baby." Then she hugged my mom.

~✦~

On Thanksgiving morning, Aunt Yolonda and her two kids, Alyssa and Kyle, came over. Alyssa was fourteen and Kyle was twelve years old. That made the weekend even better for my brothers and me because our cousins were close to us in age.

Big Mama said that before we could eat any meal, we had to go to Thanksgiving service at her church.

"It won't be a long service 'cause the pastor knows that everybody wants to go home and have dinner with their family. Don't make no sense to me to have a big ol' feast and we don't even thank the One who made it possible," Big Mama said, shaking her head.

York and Yancy weren't too excited about that but I liked Big Mama's church and couldn't wait to get there.

"Ma, I don't feel like people asking me a bunch of questions and looking at me funny," my mom said to Big Mama.

"Girl, ain't nobody studyin' you. You ain't the only one with problems, Yvette. Some folks' stuff we just know about. Everybody got somethin'. You better quit worrin' about what people think and let the Lord take care of that. If anybody got somethin' to say, tell 'em to come see me! And another thing, you and these kids need to get back in church!" Big Mama was on a roll now and once she got started it was hard to stop her.

"I work six days a week most of the time and when Sunday comes, I wanna rest, just like God did," my mom said sarcastically.

"Yvette, ain't no rest with kids. And with all you got goin' on in your house, you should be runnin' to church! I know you're tired

'cause you're doin' yo' job and Jeffery's. But what else you gon' do?
You can't let these kids loose to the streets. You gotta let God help
you raise 'em."

After that, we all went to church. Everyone enjoyed the service,
including Yancy and York. My mom even said that she wanted to
check out some churches in our area.

⟨◊⟩

"Ma, everybody don't have to go," York said as we rode in the
car to see my dad. He really wanted to have our dad all to himself.

"Well, I'm saying everybody's got to go. We're doin' this as a
family," Mom said emphatically.

"I don't know why you're making me go and see him," Yancy
said, sounding very upset.

Mom replied, "Well, you guys think you're grown and that you
run this show. But, let me tell you something—neither of you do.
I run this show. We not gon' be here long. He can only visit with
us for an hour. We're all going to see him and that's that."

It was weird. I didn't know how I felt about seeing my dad. I
wasn't superexcited like York, and I wasn't totally against it like
Yancy. Mom made it known that she wasn't overjoyed to see him.
You'd think, since she had four kids with him, that it meant she
still cared about him—right? Even though they were now divorced,
she must have loved him once.

I had seen a few prison shows where people talked to a person
through some glass. Well, that wasn't the case here. It was a nice
room. There was a couch and a table with six chairs.

A prison guard said, "Peace will be here in just a minute."

York was waiting by the door and twiddling his thumbs while

Yancy was sitting on the couch looking completely away from the door. I was sitting at the table feeling nervous. My mother was sitting beside me wringing her hands. I grabbed her hand and squeezed it.

Then I said out loud, "Lord, please bless our family."

When I said "Amen," my mother squeezed my hand back. Dad was ushered in about five minutes later wearing handcuffs. York was the first to greet him with the biggest hug after the cuffs were taken off.

"York, look at you, man," my dad said proudly.

York had this huge smile on his face and just said, "Hey, Dad."

"There's my pretty girl," my daddy said as he smiled at me. "Come here, baby."

Without thinking about how I felt, I got up out of the chair and went to hug him too.

That embrace told me how much I had missed my father. Sometimes you can't miss what you don't know you're missing. But right then I knew I was stronger with him around me. I knew with that hug that I was protected, truly loved, and special. Every girl's dream, I guess.

It wasn't every boy's dream though. When we let go, Dad looked over at Yancy. He called his name a couple of times, but he wouldn't get up.

"All right, all right, I see it's like that, huh?" Dad was trying to break the ice with Yancy.

"It is what it is," Yancy shrugged and said boldly.

"If you want to talk to the boy then you just need to cut the smart talk," my mother said. "Anyway, York is the one who wanted to see you. I hear you've been communicating with him."

"You wouldn't take my calls. I needed to talk to you guys . . . since . . . Jeff died."

"Well, you shouldn't have been here so that you could have been there. Maybe if you had been around, my baby wouldna—" Mom stopped and looked away; she couldn't finish her statement.

My dad surprised me. I remembered him having a temper. Now, he didn't get angry.

He went over to my mother and said, "You're right, Yvette. I should have been there. I've missed so much. Look at these kids. They're practically in high school already. I know our son needed me there. I'm sorry that I wasn't. I know you guys are hurting. Sometimes I cry myself to sleep in here wishing I was there to talk to that boy and let him know that it was going to be okay, but I can't go back.

"I love you guys and if I get a chance to get out of here, I'm going to do it right this time, Yvette. I'm going to be there for you all. Yvette, look at me. I'm up for parole soon. I'm gonna do better this time." Mom wouldn't turn to look at my father.

Yancy could see her face and said, "Don't cry, Ma."

"Yvette, I'm sorry," Dad said as he opened his arms and embraced Mom.

York showed all his pearly whites. "That's what I'm talking 'bout, Yancy. Daddy is trying to take care of us now. You see?"

"Ma, this is crazy," Yancy said to her as if Dad wasn't important. "You've been working two jobs since he's been in here. You're always unhappy, complaining about all that you have to do because he is in here. A pitiful 'sorry' is not enough. You might as well say he killed Jeff."

That comment struck a chord in us all. Dad let go of my mother and started toward Yancy.

"No!" my mother said, thinking that my dad's temper was about to show itself.

"I hate you, I hate you," Yancy retorted.

York got up in Yancy's face. "Why you got to do this, man? So what Dad ain't perfect. He's trying. You think everybody's got to be just perfect. We need him!"

"No, *you* need him," Yancy said.

"All right, Yancy, you need to quiet it down before the guards come in here and cut the visit short," Dad warned.

"I'm ready to go!" Yancy shouted out.

"Son," my dad said in a calmer voice.

Yancy stepped up to our dad and said, "I'm not your son."

"You're angry with me and you have every right to be. I took the easy way out to try and make good for my family; instead, it ended up backfiring on me. I got what I deserved and I'm serving my time. Like I told you when you were a little boy, never run away from your trouble—own up to it. And if it takes the rest of my life to make it up to you, Son, I'm going to do it."

My dad held his hands out for Yancy to give him love. However, Yancy rolled his eyes. Then he sat down on the couch and looked at the wall.

"So you really think they might let you out of here?" Mom asked, taking the emphasis off the tension.

"I don't know, just be praying. I do know my brother wants to help you, Yvette. Two jobs? You can't hold it down like that. I know you're stubborn. And I know you can do it without any help, but make it easier on yourself and the kids."

She looked at him like she was considering it. However, she didn't commit. Then she looked at her watch and motioned for the three of us to head out.

Dad hugged York again and told him that they would stay in touch. He kissed me on the cheek and said he loved me. Yancy didn't even look at him as he left out. I thought about what my guidance counselor had told me. She said that when you give things to God, He works them out in His time. I could only hope that would be the case for what was left of my family.

When we got back to Big Mama's house, Yancy scurried into the back room. York and I followed him. He picked up the phone.

"Who you callin'?" York asked.

Yancy said, "I'm calling Uncle John."

"Ma said she'd let us know when it was okay to call him," I said.

York said, "Yeah, we can't do it behind her back. If you want to call him then you better ask, Yancy. We don't want to upset her."

We walked into the kitchen where Mom was.

"Ma, we want to ask you something," Yancy said.

"What?" she asked.

"I want to call Uncle John," Yancy said hesitantly.

"Okay, go ahead and call him." Maybe the visit with my dad and talking with Big Mama had helped Mom to see that she needed to let God help her—through family who cared.

Thankfully, a couple of hours later, we were at Uncle John's house. We were really glad to see our other grandma, my dad's mom. It had been years since we'd visited with her. Granny, as we called her, and Big Mama had a ball talking about how life used to be "back in the day." Aunt Yolonda's family and Uncle John's family were all excited to see one another.

After catching up with what everyone had been doing, Uncle John suggested that we order some pizzas. Everybody was up for that, especially after eating so much turkey and dressing and the rest of the trimmings.

Then Uncle John called Yancy and York into his family room to talk. At first he said it was just "man talk," but then he invited me to join them.

"Listen, I know you guys are having a tough time after losing Jeff and with your dad being locked up and all. Your dad and I have talked a lot about where both of us have gone wrong in our lives. We lost Jeff but we won't lose y'all. Whatever it takes, we're gonna do it. Y'all are brothers just like me and y'all's daddy, and brothers have to take care of one another. I especially want y'all to protect ya mama and Yasmin. You feel what I'm sayin'?"

"I know what you mean," Yancy said, nodding his head.

York answered, "Yeah, me too."

"Now, I gotta go find your mama so I can talk to her," Uncle John said.

York and Yancy stayed in the family room and watched TV while I went to wash up and wait for the pizzas to be delivered. Just then I saw Mom and Uncle John talking in the hallway. I didn't mean to eavesdrop, but I was frozen from hearing their talk.

Uncle John said, "Yvette, I hope you don't feel like I'm trying to be some kind of hero. You've been the one keeping your family together all of this time. I just want to play a supportive role. My brother loves you and those kids, and he misses you guys. To be honest, he could have turned a lot of people in to shorten his time, me included. I owe him."

My mom took Uncle John's hand and said, "Thank you. Thank you for understanding. Thank you for being real and supportive. I've been stubborn too. Now I realize that I can't do it all by my-self."

Just then I moved the door and they saw me.

"Yasmin, girl."

"Sorry, Ma, I was headed to the bathroom and . . ."

Uncle John gave me a high five as he went to the door to pay the pizza deliveryman.

Mom said, "Your dad got in trouble for selling drugs. And yeah, I've been so angry at him about that and about Jeff's death. Drugs are bad news. But we can't run away from our problems. One thing your dad said that made a lot of sense is that you've got to face the bad stuff.

"Sweetheart, I owe you an apology. My growing, beautiful Yas-min Peace. I know I haven't had a lot of time for you, but I believe things will get better now. I'm glad we came. It's not all about me and what I'm going through. I'm wiser through visiting."

Chapter 10

Never
Work Out

It was now December in Jacksonville, Florida. Though the leaves had gone, you still didn't need a coat. As I walked from the bus stop to my door, the strong wind that blew around me felt refreshing. I was overcome with the need to stop having pity parties and do something to help me get better. Myreck, York, and Yancy were behind me. I didn't think they had gotten off the bus yet and I just started sprinting.

I heard Yancy call out, "Where are you going?"

I couldn't answer. I was on a mission. I couldn't put my backpack down fast enough. I went into the bedroom, fumbled through my nightstand, and started getting really frustrated.

"Why can't I find her card?" I yelled out.

I took a deep breath. "That was the last place I put it."

Thankfully, after minutes of frantically searching I found it. The piece of paper was a little bent. I straightened it out and kissed it three times.

"Yes," I said with excitement. I picked up the cordless and punched in the number. "Hello, can I speak to Miss Hall?"

"I'm sorry. She's in with clients right now. May I take a message?" the lady responded.

"No, I need to speak with her right now," I said in a determined tone.

"Honey, I'll have to take a message. She's unable to come to the phone right now. She's in a meeting."

Trying harder, I said, "No, no. She'll want to take my call. She said I was important."

"Well, I'll take a message and give it to her. I'm sure if you're as important as she says you are that she will get back to you as soon as she is available," the peppy little irritating voice replied.

I soon realized that the receptionist was not going to put me through to Miss Hall. So after I saw that I was not going to win, I gave her my name and telephone number. I was new at making a business call. I was feeling really nervous and hoping she'd call back.

"What is your message, dear?" the lady asked.

"I don't have a message. I was told to call her. She said she wanted to use me on some kind of modeling opportunity. She says it pays and all of that stuff, so I was just wondering if there were any opportunities available."

"Well, sweetheart, I can answer that. That is a *no*. You can't just call up here and get hired. Does she have your comp card?"

Confused, I asked, "What's that?"

"It's the card that contains all of your pictures, your information, and modeling experience."

"No, no. She told me that I was just one of those natural talents that she could use."

"Ha," the lady scoffed, "that rarely happens, sweetie. I get calls like this all of the time."

"Please give her my message," I said.

"Oh, I'll give her your message. I just don't think you need to be looking for a call back anytime soon. The next time we have one of those mall gigs, you should show up with the right materials if you want to take modeling serious. That's my advice to you."

"But wait—" I called out as she hung up.

I threw myself on the bed and buried my head in the pillow. I hit it with my fist several times. I thought, *I never get any breaks.*

"Hey, what's wrong with you?" York said, barging into my room.

"Leave me alone, please."

"No, I'm not going to leave you alone. You never stay out of my business. Come on. Myrek needs help workin' on his game, you down?"

"I've got homework, okay?" I sat up in the bed.

"You can do that later. Even Yancy's ready to pick up on our Harlem Globetrotter style. Come on, help him out."

"Myrek doesn't want me to help him. Trust me," I said.

"Myrek thinks he's losin' some of his edge. Trust me, he needs you, Sis. Come on." York came over to the bed and pulled me up. "Throw on some sweats and meet us on the court."

Reluctantly, I got up, changed my clothes, and jogged to the court. When we were in the fourth, fifth, and sixth grades the four of us used to make up cool basketball routines. We would do flips and acrobatic moves to make baskets. All of that energy showcased Myrek's talent most. I knew he had been in a rut for some time now. Honestly, if I could do anything to help him out of it, the way he had been there for me, I had to do it. However, that feeling changed quickly when I came out on the court and he got smart with me.

"Come on, Myrek," York said, getting in between the two of us.

Myrek said, "I'm just saying, you ain't have to get her to help."

"I don't even know why I'm out here. I've got homework to do anyway," I said as I rolled my head, eyes, and neck all at the same time.

Yancy got in my way. "The two of y'all need to kiss and make up," he said jokingly.

Quickly Myrek said, "Just like basketball, I'm blockin' that out of my head."

The ball was by my foot. I kicked it up to my hands. Then I tossed the hard, round object upside his head.

"Ouch," Myrek said, smiling at me, "fine then."

He tossed the basketball back to me. My instincts for our old habits kicked in. I did a twirl as I lifted my feet in the air and almost dunked.

"All right, all right. Now that's what I'm talkin' 'bout." York went over to his boom box and turned on some music.

Then it was on. I ran to the left and tossed the ball as Yancy ran to the right tossing the ball back to York. York spun around and tossed it to Myrek. Myrek did the prettiest dunk I had seen in a while.

When he came down, he landed straight on his bottom and said, "I don't know what's wrong with me."

"Practice, man, practice," York said as he picked him up.

We did a few other moves. Myrek just wasn't getting it. As if I was the one that caused him to fail, he palmed the ball in my face.

Rudely, Myrek said, "Thanks a lot."

Feeling hurt by that, I responded in the meanest way I could. "You're welcome a lot."

York looked at me and said, "I can't believe you. You know he needs you. I don't know why I thought this could work."

"You're just stupid, I guess," I shot back since I was really mad at him too.

I guess I wasn't as perfect as everyone thought I was. If my buttons were pushed, I could push back. Maybe I just needed to let out my frustrations as well.

⚜

Over the years, English had been one of my favorite subjects. In Literature class we had assigned seats, and I was seated in the back near two crazy boys named Tony and Nelson. We had classes together before but they never really paid me any attention. But I had to admit that over the last couple of weeks we had played and cut up more than we had done our work.

As we headed into class, Tony called out, "Wait up, Yasmin. You got to school me."

"What are you talking about?" I asked him.

Nelson came on the other side and said, "We got that big test on this Hamlet story, did you study?"

"Oh, no!" The three of us just laughed and laughed like we were watching the best comedy show around or something.

Nelson said, "So, wait a minute, you didn't turn in a paper last week. Now we have a test and you didn't study for it. Come on now, we'll get a better grade than you, girl."

"Her tests are multiple choice," I said not worrying, "certainly we'll be able to figure out what the answer is. If I get stumped, I'll just twirl my hair, and one of you guys will throw me an answer."

"Pretty hair at that," Nelson said, teasing me.

Caught off guard, I blushed. Then I saw Myrek walk by and I moved quickly away from Nelson. I had no feelings for Tony or Nelson. They were just two class clowns that I enjoyed cutting up with. I couldn't remember a year when those two guys didn't have an in-school suspension for getting on a teacher's nerves.

However, I never wanted Myrek to assume it was more than what it was. I watched him walk farther away from us. His eyes looked so sad, worse than they did the day I saw him on the basketball court when he couldn't get his game going. Even though he and I acted like we hated each other, I knew deep down we were true friends.

A part of me wanted to explain, *Oh, this isn't a big thing. It's no big deal. Please don't get upset, it's nothing.* However, I couldn't because it was time for class to begin.

"Yasmin Peace, I need to see you now," the teacher called from the front of the room.

"Oooh, somebody in trouble," Tony joked.

"Ha ha!" I got up and walked to her desk.

"Listen, young lady. You really need to get a good grade on this exam. The semester is almost over and you have a bleak outlook in my grade book. Lately you have been giving me one excuse after another. Quite frankly, it's put-up-or-shut-up time right now. All of that silly talking and joking you've been doing this semester, I hope it doesn't lead you to a big, flat flag."

I was thinking about saying, *Are you serious? I'm going to do great on this test. I always do good on your multiple-choice tests. Okay, I haven't turned in a few assignments. My class participation grades haven't been the best, but I'm going to do fine. No worries. I read enough to know what the answer isn't going to be.*

However, I could have choked when she handed me the test before I headed to my seat. It was in essay style. If I could have gone back home, studied for hours, and come back, then I would certainly do great—but I had dropped the ball. There was no way I was going to be able to get myself out of this academic slump.

Then I thought, *this is what I get.* I looked over at Tony and he was writing away; I looked at Nelson and he was doing the same. Everybody in the class was taking care of business except me. The questions must've been written in Chinese or something. I had no clue of how to even begin writing any answers.

The teacher saw me looking around and said, "I'm extremely disappointed in you."

I looked up and nodded. I could only accept it and own it. It was all my fault. Why had I been taking my schoolwork for granted? In my best subject, I was doing my worst. Report cards would be out soon, and I couldn't hide mine from my mom. I could only hope that with everything else she had going on, she would overlook it.

Throughout the rest of the day, I really felt bad. I bombed a test and upset Myrek. I couldn't wait to get to the bus and explain. When I got there and didn't see him, I asked York and Yancy where he was.

"He's not riding the bus. He made the basketball team," Yancy explained.

"Well, it's a few minutes before the bus comes. I need to tell him something right away," I said quickly.

"Girl, you gon' miss the bus and you know Ma is not coming up here to get you," York called out.

"Don't let him leave. I'll be five minutes. I'll be right back."

I ran down to the gym. As soon as I opened the door, I saw Myrek laughing with some seventh-grade cheerleader. When he looked at me earlier today, he assumed the wrong thing. But I wasn't going to misjudge what I was seeing before me. I knew I had to catch the bus, but I couldn't leave.

When he looked up and saw me staring him down, he merely shrugged his shoulders like he could care less about what I thought. Quickly, I dashed out of the gym to make it to the bus. When I took a seat, I leaned my head on the window. I wanted to at least get our friendship back on track, but there was no way that could happen now. In my crazy life, nothing was going right.

I was surprised to see my mother's car in the driveway when I got home from school. I had hoped that she wouldn't be home so that I could have our room all to myself. Wallowing in my pity was on my mind. I desperately needed to find a way to make my life a little bit happier. That was another part of my plan.

Even though she was sitting on the couch, I tried to walk past after I quickly waved to her. I didn't want her to say anything. Unfortunately for me, she instantly called me back.

"Girl, get back here. You know I am not home in the middle of my workday for my health."

"I hope I'm not next," York said, coming in behind me.

"I know the princess is not in trouble," Yancy said to me.

"Boys, does it look like I'm in a joking mood? Get to your room and do your homework. Yasmin, come here, girl."

Frustrated, I said, "Yes, Ma?"

"Your English teacher called me today," she said. I dropped my head, bummed at where this was going. "I had to call work to tell them that I would be a little late because you didn't tell me that you were failing Literature."

"I didn't know I was failing."

"Girl, don't you even try and tell me that lie. An F just doesn't come out of nowhere. She's real concerned. She told me that you were hanging with a rowdy crowd in class. How is that? Why do you find being a class clown more important than doing your work?"

I didn't have any answers, but I couldn't lie my way out of it. My mom could see through all of that. She wanted the truth. I didn't even know what the truth was. I had no explanation as to why I let my grades spiral out of control.

"Yasmin, I'm talking to you. You had a lot to say in class. Now you have your mouth closed?"

Then the phone rang and my mom answered it extremely irritated. "Hello. Hello? Yeah, this is Mrs. Peace. Yeah, this is Yasmin Peace's place of residence. Who is this? . . . a modeling agency? I don't know who signed her up for that!"

I was jumping up and down, "Mom, me, me, me!"

She then shushed me with her finger. "Well, she won't be participating."

It was the lady from the modeling agency. This was my chance to make money for the family. My mom had to understand that I could do it. I put my hands together and pleaded.

Mom turned around so that she wouldn't be facing me and finished the conversation. "Yasmin Peace won't be doin' no modeling no time soon!" Then she slammed the phone down.

"Ma," I said completely disappointed in her, "I can't believe this is my big break and you said no."

"Yeah, I said, no. Just like you said no to doing your schoolwork. How about that?"

"Ma, it'll pay money," I pleaded.

"You can't believe the half-promises some of these modeling people be promising. I don't know nothin' about this agency. Who told you to sign yourself up anyway? These folks out here are crazy."

"It wasn't like that, Ma. When I went with Veida and her mom, they didn't even choose her. The lady chose me."

"So, what, you want to take a modeling job knowing that your friend wanted it? No wonder you two have drama. What kind of friend are you?"

"You don't understand, Ma. It's not like I searched her out. The lady came after me. And when Veida found out, she thought it was cool. She said if I get in the door it would help her out.

"The two of us not talking has nothing to do with this modeling gig. It has all to do with her and Yancy. I never told her that she could spend the night over here, but she has her dad thinking that I influenced her to try and plan that. She lied on me. I know you wouldn't want me to be friends with someone who lies."

"Well, you were just standing in front of me lying about your schoolwork. You're not giving me a straight-up answer about your grades. Is it because you've been dealin' with a whole lot? And that kept you from doing your work?"

That sounded like a very rational answer to me.

"Yes," I said timidly.

"Yasmin, all I ask you to do is to keep up with your schoolwork and help me keep this house clean. Nobody's dealin' with as much as I am around here. I wish my life were better to give you guys more. I stay on you about your schoolwork because I want you to have better opportunities. I know what it's like to get caught up and not take care of your work. I've been down a road that I don't want you to travel. Okay, Yasmin?"

Mom sat down on the couch and the tears that welled in her eyes began flowing like a faucet. I desperately wanted to turn them off, but I couldn't.

"I love you, girl, and I give you everything I can. But I have limitations because of my own poor choices. Listen to me. If you don't get an education, things never work out."

Chapter 11

Better than Before

After Mom and I had our talk, my brothers came into the living room. Yancy was helping me with my Literature and York was looking over papers detailing his community service assignment. Mom was reading the newspaper.

Then the telephone rang.

I looked at the caller ID and said, "Ma, it's Mr. Ray."

Mr. Ray was the manager of our apartment building.

"I ain't got the money, so don't answer the phone. I'll deal with this," my mom said, shaking her head.

Then there was a bang at our door. "Mrs. Peace, it's Mr. Ray."

Not only was Mr. Ray calling from his cell phone, but he was standing right outside our door.

Mom opened the door with one hand and held it. "Yes, Mr. Ray?"

"Hello, Mrs. Peace. I don't want to seem like the bad guy," we heard him say, "but you're two months behind."

York bent down and said in my ear, "Man, did you know that?"

"No," I said to him.

"After all I've been through, I just need a break, Mr. Ray."

"I've got a big heart and all, Mrs. Peace. I know your son Jeff was the nicest kid around here. He always stopped to ask me what I needed without looking for me to give him anything. He was a real gentleman.

"I don't want to see you and your kids out on the street. You have a good family and I'd like to see you stay here, but you'll have to figure out a way to work this out. Out of all the families in this development, your family has given me the least trouble. But the management downtown makes these decisions, and they won't give you much longer."

"I had the rent money in full, Mr. Ray. It's just that an emergency came up and I had to use it, but I'm trying."

"Okay, you've got another week to come up with at least the past-due portion that you didn't pay last month. I want this to work out for you. I really do."

When Mr. Ray left, Mom walked to our bedroom, and my brothers and I just sat there looking at one another.

Yancy said, "Y'all, we've got to find a way to help Ma out." York and I nodded.

Though completely determined, we were unsure how we would accomplish such a task. We had to make this rent situation all good.

We needed an idea—fast.

About forty minutes later, York said to Yancy, "We're just going to have to start a little hustle. I might even be able to come up with the whole lump sum on my own."

"Are you crazy?" Yancy said to him. "You'll end up in jail like Daddy."

York charged toward Yancy. I got in between the two of them. There was no way they could be tearing at each other at a time like this. My mom was sitting in the bedroom feeling depressed. This was the last thing she needed.

Mom came to the door. "What's going on in here?"

"Nothing, Ma, nothing," I responded.

"All right. I've got to go to work and try to make some money. Please get your homework done. Stay in this house. The last thing I need is more trouble from the three of you."

"Yes, ma'am," we said.

"Yasmin, come here," she said, going back across the hall to our room.

"Yes, Ma?"

"I know Yancy was helping you earlier. Baby, I need you to keep studying. Literature is your strongest subject. You have to do better. I know you've got dreams and want to model and all that stuff. But, around here, books come first. I'm sorry I was cruel to the lady, but I do have a lot of pressure on me right now. Maybe we'll think about you being in fashion shows once those grades get better, all right?"

She gave me a big hug. I smiled.

"Okay, then. There's ramen noodles in there. Somehow we gon' get through this month," my mom said, half smiling as she walked out the door.

Jeff used to make the best ramen noodles. He was the greatest babysitter. I was his shadow. He taught me how to cook them just like he did. When the noodles were ready, I added a bit of salt and pepper and a dash of Worcestershire sauce and some American cheese. After swirling it all around, I called for my brothers to come and eat.

"Here, the phone's for you," Yancy said.

"I didn't hear it ring."

"I know, I was on it."

"Hello?"

"Is this Miss Yasmin Peace?"

"Yes."

"This is Miss Hall from the modeling agency . . . wait—I'm so sorry, I already talked to your mom. She is not allowing you to model right now. I didn't check off your name. I'm sorry. We'll talk another time."

"Wait, wait," I said desperately wanting her to hear me out.

"Yes?"

At that moment, I was so excited. I wasn't one to disobey my mom, but I didn't call the lady. She called me. Besides, I needed to figure out a way to help out with the rent.

"She said I could do it," I blurted out.

"Oh really, she seemed so determined that you couldn't earlier. What changed her mind? Is she there? May I speak to her?"

"Uhh, no ma'am. She's already left for work, but she signed the release form," I said, lying.

"Well, that's excellent. So why don't you come tomorrow to practice? The show is on Saturday and it pays three hundred dollars."

I could have choked. What a break! I was so overjoyed.

"Well, it's all set then. Please tell your mom thank you for changing her mind. See you tomorrow and you're going to do great."

When I hung up the phone, I felt really excited. Yet, I felt terrible about lying. If my mother knew she'd kill me. I had to figure out a way so that she wouldn't find out.

Then I got it! I would tell her that I had to stay after school for Literature tutoring. Of course, she would be proud because she wanted me to pull up the grade in that class anyway.

Perfect.

"Who was that?" Yancy asked.

York walked over to me to get some more noodles. "I know, it was that person that Mom said you couldn't do something with earlier."

"Shhh. Don't let Yancy hear you," I said to him.

"I feel you. You gotta do what you gotta do to help out. Yancy is Mr. Do-Everything-by-the-Book, just like Ma, and that's why we're going to be on the streets. You and me, we've got to figure out a way to make it work around here. I'll cover for you."

I desperately wanted to hug him, but that would be like admitting that scheming was the right thing to do. I was ashamed of myself, even though I was going to go through with it. But I wasn't doing it for selfish reasons. It was for my family.

I practiced for the fashion show three days straight. York covered for me while my mom believed I was staying after school for extra help.

It was a charity-event fashion show to help the homeless. Wasn't it ironic that I was really close to being there myself? However, being able to help those in need would help us stay in our apartment.

Then it was my turn to work the runway. It felt fun and free to release all of my woes and cares as I strutted with my head held high. The crowd loved me! When I was done, Miss Hall handed me an envelope.

Then she said, "I am so proud of you. You are even better than I remembered. Where's your mom? I've got to tell her thanks."

"Oh, umm she couldn't be here. You know, she works a lot."

"Oh, yeah, that's right. Well, I'll be calling her. I need to get you booked for something else. Are you going to watch the rest of the fashion show?"

"No, I really need to get home," I replied as I headed toward the exit to catch a bus.

If my mother knew I was on the public transit bus by myself, I'd be in so much trouble. I was glad it wasn't dark though. If I beat her home she wouldn't have to know.

Just as the bus approached my stop, who did I see hanging around the bus stop, smoking something more than a cigarette and up to no good—Bone and his crew.

Bone came toward me and said, "I see you coming through here wearing makeup now. Trying to be a big girl."

"I've got to get home," I said, rushing by them so they couldn't easily stop me. "Bye."

The fact that I practically had to run home was a real quick lesson in letting me know this hadn't been a good idea. But I had to. I had to help my mom. I had a check in my pocket.

I was shocked when I saw her car in front of our house. I didn't even have to wait until I got inside before she started to go off.

She came out and yelled, "Where you been?"

As we walked inside, I looked over at York, fuming for an explanation.

"I couldn't help it, Yas."

"I asked you a question, Yasmin. For the last couple of days, every time I call, your brother makes up some crazy excuse as to why I can't speak to you. I was proud, believing that you were at school tryin' to get your grades back up. I just thought I'd call you today to see if I needed to pick you up. I talked to your teacher and she said you hadn't been there none this week."

Mom lifted her eyebrows. She was waiting on me to give her an answer. Even though I really enjoyed being on the runway, I could clearly see now that it wasn't worth it at all. This wasn't one of my finest moments and it wasn't my best decision. I'd let my mom down in a huge way.

"I'm waiting, Yasmin. Give me some kind of answer, and I don't want another lie. Was I not paying you enough attention? Do you have to get into trouble like the boys? With everything I'm going through, I can't believe you're taking me through this. Where have you been, girl? I hope not with some boy!"

"No, Ma, no."

"I'm talking to you. Tell me where you've been." She was mad, but I had to show her the money.

"What are you digging for? I don't care about no paper that might be a good grade."

"Here, Ma." I handed her the envelope.

I just knew when she saw this three-hundred-dollar check that she'd forgive me. We could move on. I would not have to hear any more of her yelling.

"What is this? A modeling agency check? I don't understand, Yasmin."

"I took that gig. I was in a fashion show and I did really well. It paid three hundred dollars, Ma."

"I don't understand how this happened. I told the lady you weren't going to do it this time."

Unfortunately, my plan still wasn't working because even with my mom seeing I had made money, she wasn't letting up. She was actually getting angrier.

"You trying to tell me you went behind my back, called the lady up again, and told her you'd be in it? Even though I told her you wouldn't? And she went for that? What kind of lady is this?"

"No, no, Ma. She called back that day by accident. Then she realized that you had already said no. But she was on the phone again and Mr. Ray had come for the rent. We really needed the money. So I told her you changed your mind," I said, dropping my head and unable to even look at her.

"Get your stuff. York, hand me my purse. And, boy, if you ever lie to me again," she said.

"All right, sorry, Ma. We're just trying to help," York said, handing over her purse.

"God is going to help me," she said. "You children need to be children and let me and the Lord fix this."

"Whatever, Ma. God ain't showed up around here in a long time," York said back to her.

"Man, don't speak to Ma like that and don't talk about the Lord," Yancy said.

"Yasmin, where's this lady at?" my mom said with steam figuratively coming from her ears.

"She's at the hospital."

"The one I work in?"

"No, ma'am. The one by the mall."

"How'd you get up there to the one farther away?"

Shyly, I admitted, "I took the bus."

"What? Yasmin, all kind of fools are on public transportation."

"I know, Ma, I'm sorry. We needed the money."

"I'm going to show you how much I need this money."

When we pulled up to the hospital, the fashion show was just ending.

My mom looked crazy with her messy hair and wrinkled clothes. She hadn't even taken the time to worry about how she looked.

"Where's this lady at?"

"Mom, people haven't even been dismissed yet, please don't cause a scene."

"I need to see the lady who is in charge of all of this fashion stuff," my mom said to a lady who appeared to be involved with the fashion show.

"That would be Miss Hall. I'll let her know that you're here," the lady replied.

I got it. I had made the wrong decision. Did my mom have to embarrass me, though? Did she have to make it so I would never again be able to model with this lady? I wanted to say "I hate you" so bad, but instead tears just streamed down my face.

As we stood there waiting for Miss Hall to come, I just shook my head again. I was angry at God and thinking, *I'm trying. Why don't You help me? Why don't You make any of this work?*

When she saw Mom waiting, she said, "Yes, I'm Miss Hall." She then looked at me and continued, "Oh, Mrs. Peace, your daughter was great." Miss Hall went on and on until she realized my mother wasn't smiling about anything she had to say.

"What can I do for you? We're wrapping the show up now."

"I told you when we spoke on the phone that my daughter

couldn't participate. So take this." My mom gave her the check.

"Oh, but she told me you were fine with it. I am so sorry."

"Well, she forged my signature."

"Oh, no. Yasmin, you seem like such a sweet young lady," Miss Hall said in a disappointed tone.

My mom said, "I'll be honest, we've got some money problems, and she was trying to help me out, but I don't like her method. We need this money more than you know, but Yasmin disobeyed me by participating in the show."

"Yes, ma'am. I completely understand," Miss Hall said.

"I appreciate you taking the time to teach my daughter about the modeling thing. But I know it's a lot of slimeballs out here too. Anyway, like I told you before, it's not a good time for her to be doing this."

"Well, you take your time and let me know when it is good for her. You were adamant about your answer the first time and it seemed odd that you would change your mind so suddenly. I just took your daughter at her word. But I bear some responsibility in this matter too. Your daughter would not have been able to model if I'd done the proper thing and followed up with you.

"This fashion show benefits the homeless in the Jacksonville area and her participation was an asset to our show. Seeing a parent who is actually trying to instill values in their children is very inspiring to me. If for nothing else, please accept this check as my gift to your family."

My mom replied, "I . . . don't know what to say. Thank you, Miss Hall."

During our drive home, I thought about how even though I did something wrong, God turned it into something good. Things were actually looking better than before.

Chapter 12

Believer
Deep Within

When I got up from the altar, tears were in my eyes. I had been through so much. My family had been through a lot. I was so quick to judge God for not doing what I thought He should do in my life that I never took the time to appreciate and enjoy all the things He had done. I had my health and my strength. Though my Literature grade was not the best, it was improving. My dad wasn't physically with me but at least during the Thanksgiving holiday, I got to visit and embrace him.

I hated that I wouldn't have Jeffery here with me anymore. However, I had thirteen years of the best fun ever with him. My mom and I didn't have the best relationship, but it was getting better; and most importantly, I know she loves me. For me to still be functioning had to be because a God in heaven was looking out for me. I felt God's presence as the pastor continued to pray.

My whole family went to the altar to join the church. The pastor asked us if we had confessed Jesus Christ to be our Savior. Even though all of us had done so several years ago, York said that he didn't really understand what it meant before, but that now he did.

"Pastor Newman is pretty cool," York commented as we waited to shake his hand.

Pastor Newman's wife, my counselor, Mrs. Newman, invited my family and me to their church. My mom had said over the Thanksgiving holiday that she wanted to visit some churches in our area, so I suggested Mrs. Newman's church.

The people were very friendly and the church had activities specially designed for youth. There was a ministry for teen girls my age. I talked to the coordinator and she told me that they held meetings on Saturdays. She said some of the topics they covered were purity, dating, self-esteem, and a lot more.

I couldn't wait to sign up and get involved. I even met a couple of girls who exchanged phone numbers with me and said that if I didn't have a ride to the Saturday meetings, their parents carpooled with other parents from the church. The ministry was called G4, which stood for Girls Growing Gracefully in God.

Yancy, and surprisingly even York, talked to some of the teenage guys about some sort of adventure event just for males. My mom was excited to see them so interested.

"I am so glad to see the entire Peace family today," Mrs. Newman said as she smiled from ear to ear. You all came and joined and all I can say is, praise the Lord!"

"Thank you so much for inviting us. Thanks too for all the help that you've given Yasmin," my mom said, tearing up.

"You are so welcome. I'm glad that I could be a blessing." Mrs. Newman hugged all of us and said she'd see us at school tomorrow.

As we approached the parking lot, I heard a song coming from

someone's car. It had the most touching words: *"help me believe . . .*
I wanna believe, I'm no good on my own, please give me another chance."
I recognized one of the girls in the car, Gabrielle, who had given me
her phone number earlier.

Excitedly I asked, "Gabrielle, what's the name of that song?"

"Oh, that's 'Help Me Believe' by Kirk Franklin. I know, I love
it too!"

As Mom pulled off, we weren't going in the direction of our
home, so we wondered where we were headed. The three of us were
surprised when she turned into the parking lot of an all-you-can-
eat Sunday buffet restaurant.

"I know you guys think I ain't got enough money for this, but
I got it. I told you God was good. I got a temporary part-time job.
We gon' have a good meal and then go to the grocery store and
stock up."

"You got a new job, Ma?" Yancy asked.

"Yep, at the high school. They needed extra janitorial staff since
it's basketball season. So I'll be cleaning the gym and getting it
ready for the games. Since Jeff's old coach had an opening, he
thought of me and called. Perfect timing too. Ohhhh! I'm hungry.
Let's get something to eat."

As quick as my brothers went through the buffet lines, it
looked like there was no way they could pile all of that food on
their plates. But somehow, they managed to do it. It was so great
to be able to eat out as a family.

"You guys could have gone back for seconds," I said to them, as
my mother was still getting her plate.

"I know. I just didn't wanna get up again," York said, digging
into his mountain of food.

I just laughed. It had been a long time since the four of us enjoyed a meal out. What other cool things was God cooking up? My mom sat down with us and we prayed, even though York and Yancy had already started their feasts.

She said, "Guys, you've really been there. The best triplets ever . . . No husband . . . losing a son."

"Well, you are still married," York cut in and said.

"Boy, be quiet. I know that better than you. Y'all have been there. In your own ways you've been trying to help me out. I know you're growing up. You've got your different needs. I want the Lord to just show you His plan for your lives. Just let me stay busy working overtime trying to make ends meet for us. Again I have to say, it's my responsibility. Don't do nothin' crazy. The Lord is going to come through. We've got to believe that. You've got to have faith. Know what I'm saying?"

We all nodded. I couldn't speak for the boys, but I seriously believed what she was saying. God's ways were so much more powerful than mine. He wasn't going to leave us high and dry.

Mom put down her fork and said emotionally, "I know you've been through a lot, but I vow to make it better for my babies. I love you guys."

York got up and gave her a big kiss on the cheek. Yancy smiled. I cried and thought, *Thank You, Lord.*

⤞⤝

That wasn't all of the cool stuff He was doing. When we got home Myrek was on our steps.

"You ready to play some ball?" York asked him.

"Naw. Mrs. Peace, is it okay if I speak to Yasmin?" he asked my mom as I stood next to her.

My mom teased, "Yeah, you ain't never asked me that before. Should I be worried?"

Myrek said, "No, ma'am. Just trying to be respectful, that's all."

"Well, it's getting cold. I know it's Florida, but y'all don't need to be out here too long. Don't let the sun fool you."

"Yes, ma'am." Myrek blushed.

It actually made my insides smile for him to want to talk to me. Myrek and I went way back. With the way we'd been at each other lately, if we had any chance to make it work, this was no time for me to act like I didn't care. I didn't want it to seem like I was still mad at him.

So, in a friendly voice, I quickly said, "Hey."

Equally nice, Myrek said, "Sorry, to be just waiting here for you like this."

"No, no. What's up?"

"I just wanted to come and apologize. I've been a real jerk to you. If I'm not jealous, I'm just mad that you won't be my girl. Then I'm trying to make you jealous, knowing that I am making some other girl think I care. That's not cool. So I just came to say that, if nothing more, I do want us to be friends. Please accept my apology."

"You're not the only one who owes an apology here. I owe you one too. I know I like you; but to be honest, a part of me still wants to be a kid. I'm not ready for a boyfriend. But if I had one, it'd be you. I shouldn't ask you to wait. So I'm not going to do that."

"Well, don't ask me," he said, taking my hand from his shoulder and gripping it tight. "I want to wait. And for now can we be good friends?"

With no doubt in my mind, I knew that I now had my real true friend. We trusted each other. Only God did that. So cool.

⟨⟩

The thing I liked about being best friends with Myrek instead of a girl was that we didn't have to be together 24/7. But it also meant that a lot of times in school, I would still be alone. When I would see Asia and Perlicia together, a part of me was a little envious. Sometimes I thought of Veida.

It was so weird when she called my name. "Yasmin, do you mind if I talk to you for a second? I know you're heading to class but—"

"Sure," I said, interrupting her.

"I know I haven't been a true friend. I'm sorry you didn't approve of me being with Yancy at the dance."

Passing no judgment, I just listened. I wasn't for it. I didn't know what was wrong with me, but most of the girls around me were becoming boy crazy. Though I didn't agree to look out, I understood that I couldn't let her down even when circumstances made me.

"It wasn't your fault. It was mine. A friend shouldn't ask a friend to do something wrong. And I shouldn't have led my dad to believe that the whole spending the night at your house thing was your idea. I so miss you, Yasmin. Some of the girls at school have tried to be my friends and they all get on my nerves. I always wonder about you and what you're doing."

"It's okay," I said. "For a long time I had been holding a grudge. I'm not perfect. Why should I expect you to be? I had the nerve to be mad at God. I believe He has forgiven me. I need you to do the same."

"I feel so much better. Thank you." She clasped her hands together. "So, we're best friends again?"

As she hugged me real tight, I quickly said, "Well, how about good friends? Let's just go slowly."

I had to put a disclaimer out there. No need to set our friendship bar too high. It was just a good thing that we were talking.

***

"Kids, I'm home," Mom said about eleven o'clock that night.

The management office had just left us another notice about our rent. We needed to do something so that we wouldn't get evicted. York looked at me and I looked at Yancy. None of us wanted to tell her the bad news, but someone had to.

So I said, "Mom, we have another rent notice."

"I know, baby."

"So, what are we going to do?" Yancy asked.

"Well, I have an idea. I'll need you all to help Mama out, though."

York stood and clasped his hands. "That's what I've been trying to do. All you have to do is say the word. I can get some cash."

"And I can call Uncle John," Yancy cut in.

"Thank you, boys, but that's not what I mean. The coach at the high school needs entertainment for the game. He's going to pay three hundred dollars. I was thinking, if y'all could get with Myrek and do that Harlem Globetrotter routine y'all used to do, we'll have the money. The crowds always went wild for that. You think Myrek will do it?"

York and Yancy looked at me. I shook my head at them both. They were so silly implying he'd do anything for me.

York said, "Yeah, he'll do it."

"Yeah, for his best friend," Yancy said, smiling at me.

"Whatever. We're good friends." I playfully rolled my eyes at him.

"All right, 'best or good friends,' you'd better watch it, young lady," my mom cautioned.

"Ma, I'm serious. It's nothing like that going on."

"Yeah, right," York teased.

"Ma!"

"I believe you, Yasmin," she said, smiling.

❦

The game was going great and everyone was having a ball. Myrek was wowing the crowd and the rest of us did pretty good too.

It was halftime so I decided to go to the concession stand and get some nachos.

"What's up, girl?" Bone said. "I've got to chase you down and stuff. I told you, you owe me a debt for your brother. What do I need to do to prove it to you?"

Lord, I thought. *Please help me. I am so scared right now.*

From out of nowhere, York stepped in between the two of us. "Wait a minute, man. What you sayin' to my sister?"

"Oh, you gon' do something about it?" Bone said.

"If I have to I will," my brother stepped to him and said.

"He says he'll hurt you if I don't work for him and that Jeffery owed him some kind of debt," I told York.

"What? Man, how you gon' play us like that? That's what you told me. I told you I'd work for you. But you know what? I'm smarter than that."

Just then the best thing that could've happened—did.

I looked up and shouted, "Uncle John!"

"What's goin' on? Is there a problem here?" Uncle John walked up and asked. Yancy followed close behind.

"Hey, Uncle John," York said, looking really shocked.

Pointing to Bone, York said, "I saw him sayin' something to Yasmin so I came over to look out for her. He's tellin' her that she owes him somethin' because of Jeff. Honestly, Uncle John, at first I had agreed to hustle for him, but I know that's not right."

"Let me tell you something," my uncle said to Bone, "the Peace kids don't owe you nothin'. If there is any kind of debt to be paid, come see a man about it. And that man is me. No more conversations with my niece and nephews. Understood?"

Bone mumbled something, shook his head, and walked away. I could tell he didn't know what to think.

Uncle John said to York, "I see you were protectin' your sister just like I told you a man does. I told your mama I was gonna surprise you all and come to this game. I'm glad I found you doin' the right thing."

That was a great surprise.

Everything was working out. Mom made the money that we needed for rent and things couldn't have been better.

⌘

Later that night, I called over to Myrek's house and heard someone crying in the background before I even heard a hello. "Myrek, it's me, Yasmin."

"Yasmin, hold on."

"What happened? You need to call me back?" I asked.

"No, wait. I'm goin' into another room so I can talk," he said. "It's Jada."

"What about her?" I held my breath.

"She's pregnant."

"Pregnant? For real?" I exclaimed.

"What? Who?" York was listening in the background.

"You can tell him," Myrek said.

I explained, "Myrek said that Jada is pregnant."

"What did you say, Yasmin?" Mom asked.

"Ma, Myrek said Jada is pregnant," I repeated the news.

"Oh, Jesus," Mom said, praying.

"My dad said to ask your mom to come over if she can," Myrek went on.

"Ma, Myrek's dad wants to know if you can come over?"

"Tell him I'll be right there, Yasmin," she said as she quickly put on her shoes and grabbed her Bible. Even though this was a tough situation, seeing my mom grab a Bible was a good thing.

"Honestly, Yasmin, I don't know, but I can at least see what you were saying. We are too young to move too fast."

I was glad that Myrek understood.

When my mom returned she sat us down and told us that Jada said that she was pregnant by Jeff.

Mom said that we would get through this situation. We could lean on each other, our extended family, and even our church family. But more importantly—God.

She said we should begin praying for Jada, her family, and the unborn baby.

A few months back I had little faith in God working things out for my good. Though I kept on going, things got even crazier. Now that I'd gotten through storms, I could clearly see that God didn't leave me. He was there caring for me, leading me, and guiding me. All I had to do was trust Him, even when I couldn't see the way. Now that I had more than just faith the size of a little seed, I knew I was a believer deep within.

Acknowledgments

I wrote this Yasmin Peace series because I deeply care for the young teen struggling in the inner city. Whether you are a teen practically raising yourself, desperately down because of your circumstances, or praying for money so you can help your family survive, I wanted you to know God will see you through. Life is worth living.

It's easy to let the tough situations weigh you down, but I hope this book encourages you to look for the good and stay upbeat. When you have a great attitude and seek God's help, your dark day will brighten. Though you might not have everything you want, know God has given you everything you need.

Always remember He is the way. Here is a shout out of thanks to the folks who have helped me keep the faith and stay on my novel-writing journey. When you find your faith, you'll understand you're not in it alone.

For my family, parents Dr. Franklin and Shirley Perry, Sr.,

brother, Dennis and sister-in-law, Leslie, my mother-in-law, Ms. Ann and extended family, Rev. Walter and Marjorie Kimbrough, Bobby and Sarah Lundy, Antonio and Gloria London, Cedric and Nicole Smith, Harry and Nino Colon, and Brett and Loni Perriman, your support helped me find and use my voice.

For my publisher, Moody/Lift Every Voice, and especially my editor, Tanya Harper, your diligence helped me find and keep the balance.

For my 8th grade friends, Veida Evans, Kimberly Brickhouse Monroe, Joy Barksdale Nixon, Jan Hatchett, Vickie Randall Davis, and especially Amber Jarrett, who left us too early, (Girl, we miss you, but we know God needed you), your long-lasting friendships helped me find and tell better stories.

For my sorority, Delta Sigma Theta, especially, Dr. Lousie A. Rice, your humbling recognition of me as the 2008 Emerging Artist award winner helped me find and maintain encouragement.

For my children, Dustyn Leon, Sydni Derek, and Sheldyn Ashli, your dependence on me helped me find and understand what truly makes me full.

For my husband, Derrick Moore, your love for me helped me find and cling to the joy only living life with a best friend can bring.

For my readers, practically those who don't have life easy, your broken hearts helped me find and dig to bring forth a message that I hope will lift your soul.

And for my precious Lord and Savior who is daily teaching me that only He is equipped to fight our battles, Your grace and mercy helped me find and live out my true purpose for living.

Discussion Questions

1. Yasmin Peace's family is dealing with the terrible loss of her older brother. Do you feel the way the family is handling their grief is helping the family heal? What are some things to do to help a person cope with death?

2. Asia and Perlicia are mean to Yasmin at school. Do you think Yasmin's response to their negative comments is appropriate? Explain ways that the Lord would like you to deal with people who give you a rough time.

3. Bone, the neighborhood bully, threatens Yasmin. Do you believe Yasmin was right in keeping this encounter to herself? Who are people you can trust in your life to help you handle very dangerous situations?

4. Yancy is tired of being called a geek and York hates that he doesn't have any new clothes. Do you agree with how Yasmin's brothers deal with their insecurities? What would you do if you felt like you wanted a big part of your life to change?

5. Veida really wants to have a model frame like Yasmin, and Yasmin really wants to have a home like Veida. Is it good that

they both talked about what was in their hearts? What are ways you can make sure you don't get envious of your friends?

6. At the fall party, Yasmin and Veida fall out. Do you think it was Yasmin's fault that Veida and Yancy got caught by the teachers? Do you feel God expects you to help others get out of trouble?

7. York steals from the store and their mom is devastated. Do you think he was right to try and get new clothes by any means necessary? How can you stay away from things that tempt you?

8. Myrek asks Yasmin to be his girl. Do you think he should be mad at her when she says no? Is it better to please a guy/girl or God?

9. The Peace family goes to visit their dad in jail. Do you think Yancy is right to be very angry his dad made bad choices? What are ways you can build up a broken relationship?

10. The model agent wants Yasmin to be in her program, but her mother won't allow it because Yasmin has bad grades. Do you think her mother is being too harsh? How can two people strive to both get the same goal without tearing down the dreams of the other?

11. The landlord needs his money for the rent. Do you think it is all three kids' responsibility to help their mother get the bills paid? What are ways a teenager is expected to do his or her part to help their parents?

12. Jada, Jeff's former girlfriend, is having his baby. Do you think this is a good or bad thing? What are some ways God has taken the wrong things in your life and made it right?

Stay tuned for the next book in this series,

Believing in Hope

Yasmin Peace Series Book 2

Stephanie Perry Moore

available February 2009, wherever books are sold.

Until then, enjoy the following excerpt
from the life of Yasmin Peace.

Chapter 1

Stronger Each Day

"Yasmin, you and your brothers need to come over to my house right now," Myrek said to me over the phone with great urgency in his voice.

"Huh? What are you talking about?" I said to my next-door neighbor and best buddy of many years.

I was really confused about why he sounded panicked. My mom had just come back from Myrek's apartment. Mr. Mike, Myrek's dad, had asked her to come over to discuss the situation about Jada, Myrek's sister. My brother, Jeffery Jr., whom everybody called Jeff, used to date Jada. Well, now Jada said that she is pregnant—and that Jeff was the father!

Though my brother York wasn't at all happy about it, my other brother Yancy and I certainly thought this was great news. I wasn't naïve or anything. I know that it is not God's plan for a teenage girl to be unwed and pregnant. But because of what my grandma always said could come out of a mess, I had hope that God would bring a miracle into these circumstances. After explaining the situation to my brothers and me, Mom realized that she'd left her Bible at Myrek's house, so she went back to get it.

"Yas, please don't ask me no questions. Seriously, could y'all come on over here?" Myrek said, as I heard loud talking behind him.

My mom was over there cutting up. Why though? She had just said that we needed to be prayerful and God would work everything out. It had only been months since Jeff took his own life. Just when I was getting over the fact that I would probably lose every connection I ever had with him, I find out that I will have a niece or nephew, keeping a part of Jeff in this world. What could possibly be going wrong now?

Quickly, I slid on my slippers and hung up the phone without saying bye.

I looked at York and Yancy. "Let's go. Mom's over there showing out."

"I told y'all this isn't our fight. This isn't our business," York said, not wanting to get up out of his seat. "Jada is too young to have a baby. Besides, whatever that girl wants to do with her body ain't got nothing to do with us."

"Yeah. Like Jeffery would want her to kill the baby?" Yancy said to York. "We gotta be his voice. We gotta do whatever we can to make sure she knows that she's not in this alone. So get up and let's go over there. Now!"

I couldn't believe Yancy grabbed York's collar. I knew that wasn't going to go over well. The two of them started pushing and shoving each other back and forth. It was just killing me how every five minutes they were getting into it about something.

"Guys, this isn't about us. Mom is over there fussing with Myrek's dad. Can't we just keep whatever we feel to ourselves and go bring Mama home?"

York said, "Mama's grown. What about this don't you understand?"

"I understand that she's our mom and obviously it's a big enough deal that Myrek thought we could help by being over there. It's not like I'm putting my nose into something that I'm supposed to stay out of. We were basically asked to come over and help. If you want to sit here and do nothing, or if you two want to stay here and argue, then fine. I'll go by myself." I opened our apartment door and stood in the doorway.

"I'll go," York said, knowing that I made a very valid point.

The front door of Myrek's apartment was wide open.

"You just can't go around giving no demands, Yvette," Mr. Mike said to our mom. "Jada is my daughter. She's going to do what is best for her. All of us are struggling in these projects. We're barely able to take care of the kids we got now. You workin' two jobs. I'm working seventeen hours.

"How we gonna be able to take care of a grandchild? And your son ain't even here to help. I'm sorry if this hurts. I'm sorry if I'm saying the tough stuff, but I'm being real. Jeff's gone and we need to move on. Jada has a future that includes finishing school. And having a baby just ain't a part of that future."

My brothers and I were standing behind our mom.

"You not gon' tell me that y'all gon' deal with this without me!" Mom said, fussing. "Are you tellin' me that she's not gonna have the baby?"

Finally he said, "Y'all need to get your mom up on out of my apartment. This is my daughter and we gon' deal with it how she needs to."

No one seemed to notice that Jada was in the corner crying. Our parents just kept going back and forth at it. They were getting so loud and crazy that obviously this girl could not take any more of it. Suddenly, she ran outside and I followed her.

"Jeffery, why'd you have to leave me? I'm sorry I told you it was Bone's baby. I just thought it would be better. I didn't want to mess you up and keep you from going on to college. I didn't know you were gonna take it so hard. Please forgive me, God. Please forgive me!" Jada sobbed.

I was going out there to console Jada, but hearing what she said made me stop as if I'd come to a stop sign and a policeman was waiting to give me a ticket if I proceeded. And then when I was able to move, when I could go forward to comfort her, it was like my car broke down. How could I comfort a girl who basically was confessing to the fact that she was probably the reason why my brother took his own life?

Now granted, I found out that he owed Bone money for not throwing the high school state championship game. I'd also learned that his grades were horrible and he probably wasn't going to get a chance to go to college after all. But I still knew Jeff to be so strong. None of that made me think he'd be that down. But this? I believe that he loved Jada. If she told him that she was having someone else's baby, he would have been devastated. I screamed to release my pent-up frustration.

Jada turned around and said, "How long have you been standing there?"

· "Long enough," I said with one hand on my hip. "Why'd you lie to my brother?" I demanded.

"I don't know. I thought I was doing the right thing. I thought I could pull this off. I didn't think he would end everything. I was fooling myself that Jeff wouldn't care. Please, please forg—"

Getting close to her face, I snarled and said, "Please what? My brother's gone. We don't have no real reasons or answers why he did what he did. If you told him this terrible lie, then of course he felt helpless and weak. How could you? And you don't even know if you want the baby!"

Jada looked at me with tears streaming down her face and said, "Yasmin, you have no clue about what I'm going through!"

I was overcome with the sick feeling grief brings. At that point, I ran back to my own apartment. Sitting on my bed that I shared with my mom, I rocked back and forth.

Lord, I thought I knew You were there. You've proven to me that You care about me, but why does each day seem to be harder? Why can't I just feel good? Why can't I just get good news? Why can't I be a normal eighth-grade girl? Drama free?

"Wait a minute. I'm not taking no handouts from nobody. What's all this food for?" I heard Mom say in an irate way.

I was surprised to see my counselor and pastor's wife, Mrs. Newman, and my Algebra teacher, Miss Bennett, at our apartment. They said they had come on behalf of the *Reach Out and Touch Ministry* from our church. The baskets of food they brought sure smelled good. So good that my brothers had come out of their bedroom.

"Mom, what you sayin'? We hungry," York said to her as his eyes got really wide, staring at all of the food.

"Boy, I told you, you might be getting bigger but you are not grown up in here. I didn't ask for no handouts. I don't want no handouts. Thank y'all very much, but go to somebody else's house. The lady next door, Sandra, got two little kids. And believe it or not, she's struggling worse than me. Take the food to her."

"Mom!" I said, feeling really embarrassed that my mother had such pride. My grandma had fussed at her about being too prideful to accept help. She couldn't even accept a blessing.

The first time that we visited the church, Pastor Newman's message moved my whole family and we joined the church. Then the minister over the new members' ministry explained to us the importance of not only being a member but of having a relationship with Jesus Christ. Mom even left the service saying that she was happier than she'd been in a long while.

"Mom, how come we can't accept it?" I asked.

"Because—in case you forgot, Yasmin Peace, I'm the one who makes decisions up in here," she said sharply.

They were being nice to us and bringing us a meal when, truth be told, earlier in the day Mom was trying to figure out what we were gonna eat. I could understand not wanting to take handouts if you didn't need it, but she'd already said we were struggling. She had two jobs and was still behind on the rent and utilities. Coupled with the way my brothers ran through the food stamps, we needed help.

Mrs. Newman said, "You know, I'm sorry, Mrs. Peace. The church wasn't trying to make you feel like you can't do this. We know you didn't ask for a handout. It's just that this is the end of the holiday season and we'd like to bless grieving families who have suffered a severe loss. This is just a little something to start the New Year off with a victory."

Miss Bennett stepped forward and said, "Yes, she's right. So many people get so much during the time when they actually lose a loved one, but after that, sometimes they still need folks to come by and show them some love. That's what we're all about."

Mrs. Newman chimed back in and said, "We can imagine the holidays had to be tough, but we were praying for you guys. If you need anything, the church is here to help. Please take this ham, fried chicken, green beans, rice, macaroni and cheese—"

"Aw, come on, Ma. You gotta let us get that," York said.

"Shut up, boy!" she said to him. "Go sit down."

"And we've got black-eyed peas," Mrs. Newman continued. "Can't start the New Year off without black-eyed peas. If you prefer us to take this food next door to your neighbor, we can do that. But we'd certainly love to give it to you all. Maybe you can invite your neighbors over here to share with you. There's plenty enough."

Mom looked at my brothers who were practically drooling like they couldn't wait to tear into the food. Then she looked over at me and saw that I was a little salty because she had sort of embarrassed me in front of our visitors.

Then she said calmly, "Just so you know, this isn't a handout. We appreciate it. Kids, let's put everything in the kitchen."

We laid the spread on the kitchen table. My brothers were smiling from our place in Jacksonville all the way to Miami.

Before Mrs. Newman and Miss Bennett left, they asked if we could circle up in prayer and thank God for His many blessings. My mom said that was a great idea; my brothers, who acted as if they hadn't eaten in years, reluctantly grabbed hands.

We walked over to the table and Mom just hugged me. "Thank you, baby," she said as she gave me a kiss on my forehead.

"For what?" I said still having a slight attitude.

"Just because. Just because."

Maybe I did need to keep trusting God. Maybe He was working in my mom's heart after all. Though I was still so bummed out with her, I had to force a smile on my face because of her change of heart. It sure felt good having her arms around me. Something was definitely working.

"Ooh, this sure is a lot of food," Mom said after Mrs. Newman and Miss Bennett left. "Yas, why don't you go next door and see if Miss Sandra is at home."

"Yes, ma'am," I said and headed to her apartment. As I approached the door, I didn't even have to knock; I could tell there was no one home because it was so quiet. Usually, you could hear the kids playing and making noise inside their apartment. Besides, her car wasn't parked outside in its usual spot.

Miss Sandra was an interesting character. She had two young kids: a five-year-old daughter, Randi, and a son, Dante, who was almost two. She worked at the grocery store stocking items on the shelf, and she also worked nights at a second job.

Back last spring, I remember when she and my mom got into it. Mom had caught her leaving the kids at home alone while she was out trying to make ends meet. When Mom threatened to call the Department of Children and Family Services, also known as DCFS, Miss Sandra just broke down. Ever since then, my mom was trying to do all she could to help the lady. We watched the kids, and we shared our food with them.

But after Jeff died, Mom just shut out all that helping others. One day I heard her mumbling that she could barely help her own children. How was she going to help someone else raise theirs? After that, we didn't know who was taking care of her little babies, but I knew my mom still cared about them.

"They're not there, Ma," I said, coming back to our apartment.

Then she put on her shoes.

"Where you going?" York said to Mom. "We 'bout to eat. You gotta go to work, but can't you even eat with us?"

"Boy, calm down and mind your own business. Y'all set the table and warm up the food. I'm grown, don't ask me no questions," she said.

Yancy cracked open the door to find out where Mom was going; surprisingly, she went right to Myrek's house.

My brothers and I stood in the doorway eavesdropping.

"I'm sorry things got a little out of control the other day, Mike," my mom said. "I have some food. It's New Year's Day and every-body deserves a good meal. Would you and the kids like to come over and eat with us?"

"Yvette, why would we want to do that? You're trying to tell my daughter what she's got to do with her baby."

"No, it's not gonna be none of that. I learned my lesson. Though I got strong views, I've just been praying about it. Some stuff I can't fix, like my husband being in jail when I need him, you know? You just gotta learn how to roll with the punches and move on."

"See, why she gotta be talking about Dad to him?" York said as the three of us listened. "I don't want them coming over, eating our food. We got a refrigerator that's empty. We can have leftovers and grub for days. I sure hope he says no."

"Quit being selfish," I said to York.

"Yas just wants Myrek to come over here, Yancy," York said, getting under my skin like a bad rash.

"Yeah, she just wants Myrek to come over here," Yancy teased as he messed with my hair.

I wasn't even thinking like that. Myrek and I were cool with each other. We decided we had some feelings for each other, but we just want to be friends. We weren't trying to have nothing serious going on.

My two brothers had their issues. I still couldn't believe that Yancy hated being smart and detested being teased by his peers so much that he started getting bad grades just so he wouldn't have to take accelerated classes. And finally he gets a girlfriend, Veida Hatchett. She was supposed to be my friend but had dropped me the first time I didn't like her being so fast with my brother.

And York wasn't any better, wanting to act like we had more than we did. He felt the need to dress in the fliest clothes so bad that he was willing to steal for them. Then he was arrested and had to perform community service.

Both of those things were stressing my mom out so bad. And then for her to find out that there's a chance that a part of my oldest brother could still be here on earth made her wrestle at night. I'm sure that's why she was unable to sleep at night; she was carrying so much on her. Yet she treated me like I was a kid and wouldn't talk to me like a friend who could take some of this stuff off of her. But I do feel bad that even though I didn't want to show her any resistance, I still gave her lip—more than she deserved.

"Let's get ready for our guests, y'all. Mom asked us to get the food ready. Let's just do it, okay?" I told them.

"You act like they're comin'," York said.

"Mom's over there asking them," Yancy said. "What else are they eating? They're just like us. Poor, trying to make it. They'll be over here for some food."

Sure enough, ten minutes later my mom came through the door with Mr. Mike, Myrek, and Jada. Myrek and I looked at each other with such awkwardness. We had been best friends since forever. But why did it feel different now? Maybe it was just because we were growing up. I thought he looked quite handsome in his new sweater that he must've gotten for Christmas—but I wasn't going to tell him that.

Teasing him, I said, "Make sure you don't eat up all the chicken legs. You know that's my favorite part."

Myrek said, "I'm glad your mom came over. My dad was fixing chicken noodle soup."

Jada said, "Hey, Yasmin."

I remembered the last time I had seen her, she was confessing that she had really hurt Jeff with some of the things she'd said to him. At that moment, I thought I could never forgive her. But then it was as if God pinched me. I had to move past this.

I said, "Can I talk to you for a second?"

"I'm really not up to it, Yasmin. I just can't deal with the stress. My dad and your mom have talked about this enough. I really want a good meal and then I'm going back to bed."

"I'm not gonna stress you out, but I do want to talk to you. Mom, we'll be right back," I said, heading to my bedroom. I wasn't taking *no* for an answer.

Sitting down on my bed, Jada said, "Okay. What? I was wrong and I'm sorry."

"Well, I'm sorry too for acting all high and mighty like I was judging you. I know you didn't mean for Jeff to go over the edge. He made that decision for himself. I guess I just wanted to let you know that I don't hold you responsible. That's all."

Looking surprised, Jada said, "Thanks, Yasmin." We hugged and then she and I headed to the kitchen.

Just then, I heard Mom and Myrek's dad laughing. For two people who weren't getting along a few days before, they were certainly acting chummy now.

"This ain't even gonna happen and go down like that," York said.

"What?" I asked.

"Myrek and Yancy are talking about getting the two of them together. That is not gonna happen as long as I'm here. No way."

I didn't know how I felt about that, even though my parents were divorced. With the divorce and my dad still being in jail, it didn't mean that he and my mom couldn't get back together when he got out. Mom had made a lot of sense when she said some stuff wasn't for us kids to get into. But whatever Myrek's dad was saying to her, it sure felt good to see her smile. The meal was a blessing to both of our families.

When I returned to school after the Christmas break, I thanked my Algebra teacher, Miss Bennett, for coming by to help my family. I also went to my counselor's office to thank her and to just talk.

"Mrs. Newman, I'm sorry that my mom didn't want to accept the help at first." Needing to vent, I went on, "You just don't even know. She is so strong. She does it her way, but it's like I don't even have any say over anything. Like she doesn't care at all what I think. Sometimes I get so tired of her acting like that. I don't have any hope that she's ever going to change and see me as the young woman I'm trying to be. Lately, York and Yancy have made bad choices. Then with my brother, Jeff, taking his own life—it's been really hard on her."

She touched my shoulder and said, "Listen, Yasmin, you just told me she's going through a lot. Don't lose hope in her. I believe your relationship will get better. You and your whole family will bounce back stronger from all that you had to deal with last year.

"Most people we minister to act as if they think they deserve stuff just being given to them. Your mom's not like that. She has integrity. She wants to provide and take care of her kids. She may seem overprotective, but she's just a mama bear who's had some cubs wander a little too far away. And your mom knows that you haven't, she just wants to do everything in her power to make sure you don't stray. There's love, honor, and strength in her."

I told Mrs. Newman about the drama between Myrek's family and mine and how my mom went over there with her Bible and then ended up really getting into it with Mr. Mike. Then later Mom invited the family over to share the dinner that the church had blessed us with.

"Well, Yasmin, as you can see, just because a person is a Christian doesn't mean they don't get angry and maybe say or do some things they wish they hadn't. The important thing is that your mother extended herself to another family despite the conflict between you all. I'd say that your mom is really demonstrating the love of Christ—even in her own pain. And at the very least, thank God that she took the Bible with her!"

We had been through so much. And we weren't totally healed; the pain and the loss of Jeffery still hurt so badly. I had no idea what would happen with Jada, and I worried about York and Yancy going through their own tough times. I also had major concerns about my mom trying to keep our family on track.

Through it all, thankfully, God hadn't forgotten the Peace family. We were getting stronger each day.

THE PAYTON SKKY SERIES

From her senior year of high school to her second semester of college, this series traces the life of Payton Skky, showing how this lively and energetic teenager's faith is challenged as she faces tough issues.

 MOODY
PUBLISHERS.

1-800-678-8812 · MOODYPUBLISHERS.COM

The Negro National Anthem

Lift every voice and sing
Till earth and heaven ring,
Ring with the harmonies of Liberty;
Let our rejoicing rise
High as the listening skies,
Let it resound loud as the rolling sea.
Sing a song full of the faith that the dark past has taught us,
Sing a song full of the hope that the present has brought us,
Facing the rising sun of our new day begun
Let us march on till victory is won.

So begins the Black National Anthem, by James Weldon Johnson in 1900.
Lift Every Voice is the name of the joint imprint of The Institute for Black
Family Development and Moody Publishers.

Our vision is to advance the cause of Christ through publishing African-
American Christians who educate, edify, and disciple Christians in the
church community through quality books written for African-Americans.

Since 1988, the Institute for Black Family Development, a 501(c)(3) non-
profit Christian organization, has been providing training and technical assis-
tance for churches and Christian organizations. The Institute for Black Family
Development's goal is to become a premier trainer in leadership development,
management, and strategic planning for pastors, ministers, volunteers, execu-
tives, and key staff members of churches and Christian organizations. To learn
more about The Institute for Black Family Development write us at:

The Institute for Black Family Development
15151 Faust
Detroit, Michigan 48223

We hope you enjoy this book from Moody Publishers. Our goal is to provide
high-quality, thought-provoking books and products that connect truth to
your real needs and challenges. For more information on other books and
products written and produced from a biblical perspective, go to www.
moodypublishers.com or write to:

Moody Publishers/LEV
820 N. LaSalle Boulevard
Chicago, IL 60610
www.moodypublishers.com